# THE ROGUE THREAD

## GRACE HUDSON

This edition published in 2017
Copyright © Grace Hudson
All rights reserved.

The moral right of the author has been asserted.

ISBN-13: 978-1977597076
ISBN-10: 1977597076

Printed and bound by Createspace
DBA of On-Demand Publishing, LLC
www.createspace.com

Cover Design by Sanura Jayashan
Interior Formatting by GH Books

Sign up to the Grace Hudson newsletter:
www.gracehudson.net
Twitter: @gracehudsonau
Facebook: www.facebook.com/gracehudsonauthor
Goodreads: www.goodreads.com/gracehudson

This edition is also available in e-book
978-1-68418-189-6

*This book is dedicated to my partner.*
*He knows why.*

# 1

Operator Quinton tapped the screen of his cracked monitor, the power stuttering as the image dimmed and brightened. The night was still and the moon provided only a dim source of light, with only a thin crescent visible above the tree line. Quinton had begun to squint and his eyelids were heavy from staring at the monitor. The young Operator checked his timepiece, noting the time of 20:00. Another thirty minutes and he would be back in his chambers sleeping after the long spell of watch duty. His eyes snapped open when a faint boom sounded in the distance.

He sat back in his chair, rubbing his eyes. Many evenings were spent listening to the various rattles and booms from the different levels of Fertility Emigration Resource and Training Supply, or FERTS. He had asked Officer Cerberus for an explanation after a particularly loud roar some evenings back. Cerberus had attributed the sound to one of the furnaces. Quinton had never seen the furnaces for himself as he lacked the necessary clearance, but Cerberus had briefly explained that due to their age, the furnaces were prone to malfunction, much like the power supply.

Quinton believed he had a basic understanding of the difficulties faced by the complex. Traditional petroleum fuel was so scarce that it was now disregarded as a viable source of energy. FERTS ran on a system of linked solar panels, with the excess energy diverted to battery storage for night use. The backup generators contained a diesel hybrid, a remnant from the days before the war. The generators were rarely used, and the Operators were under strict instruction never to use the backup generators unless absolutely necessary. According to his superior, Officer Cerberus, once the remaining fuel supply was exhausted, the backup generators would be rendered useless.

Quinton sighed, tapping his monitor once more. He was certain there had been another distinct sound, marking the time at 20:03. The furnaces were well stocked with wood, supplied by the labor of Kappa circuit, but he supposed there was no predicting the nature of the furnaces once they were in use. If Officer Cerberus considered the sounds of the furnace to be routine, then he supposed he would learn to ignore them, along with the fluctuations in the power supply. He shook his head, tapping at the monitor again to bring up the image on his screen.

There had not been a disturbance since the attempted escape of Beth 259251 some months ago, and the Ward Beacon had been efficient in expiring the Epsilon Internee. A short charge of electricity activated by the Ward Beacon had sparked through her implant marker and rendered her immobile before her heart gave out. Quinton shivered, the memory unpleasant, though he should have been used to it by now. On the direction of Pinnacle Officer Wilcox, the Ward Beacon was the only security measure required to rein in any attempts at escape. The Ward Beacon was effective as an escape deterrent, and this pleased Officer Cerberus, which in turn pleased Quinton. That was all that mattered.

He checked his timepiece. The time read 20:05. Scanning the darkness, he searched for any sign of movement from his vantage point. The tower afforded a view of the tree line and the plains of the suspension zone, though little else was visible from this height. Quinton scanned the tree line once more, finding nothing. The monitor had not detected the signature of any implant markers outside the designated areas within the complex. He busied himself with filling in his log entries for the day, as Pinnacle Officer Wilcox insisted on precision in all records.

Another explosion sounded, jolting Quinton from his logs. The lights on his monitors flickered and faded to black. The overhead lighting cut out, leaving him in temporary blackness. The tree line was clearer now, the thin sliver of the moon watching over the rocky outcrops of the vast suspension zone.

The overhead lighting hummed, switching to the dull blue glow from the backup generator. Quinton tapped his monitor, brushing the thin layer of dust from the screen. This time, the monitors remained blank.

He reached for his radio but decided against it, reminded of Officer Cerberus' instructions to restrict all use unless absolutely necessary. It was yet another restriction for Quinton to incorporate into his daily track and surveillance duties. The batteries for the radios were finite, and though a stockpile had been accumulated through Pinnacle Officer Wilcox's military contacts, their use was to be limited to official duties such as maintenance and Internee escape attempts.

Quinton checked the tree line once more, finding no signs of movement in the blackness, though visibility was next to nothing. Without the monitor, line of sight with the naked eye was essentially useless. He tapped the monitor with his fingertips. The monitors remained blank. He checked the wires beneath the console, affirming connections were secure. The Ward Beacon's sensors had detected no movement from the Internees and no implant markers outside the ward zone had activated the siren. The beacon operated on the same radio frequency as the implant markers, injected below the collarbone of each Internee around the time of birth. In the event of an escape, the Ward Beacon's sensors detected the location of the implant marker outside the ward zone and engaged the siren. An Internee was afforded a total of six minutes to return to the ward zone once the siren was mobilized. Historically, few had been prepared to take such a risk.

The Ward Beacon provided a colossal drain on

power for the complex, most of its time spent in standby mode to conserve resources. Once the beacon was set in motion, statistics were engaged, feeding to the monitors various particulars such as Beth number, Y number determined by days since birth, and basic endurance data such as respiration and heart rate, yet none of these features had appeared on his screen. Quinton sighed, leaning back in his chair. This would not do. He would have to log the malfunction. Officer Cerberus frowned upon any kind of interruption to an Operator's routine track and surveillance duties, and he had already displeased his superior Officer on more than one occasion.

He fumbled for his radio, pressing the button as the static hissed to life.

"Monitor malfunction, observation tower. Time of malfunction 20:05."

Operators were instructed to keep radio broadcasts concise. Quinton resisted the urge to converse with the maintenance Officers, his only form of contact with others on this seemingly unending shift.

"Negative, Quinton," said the familiar voice, crackling through the static. "Priority maintenance at Pinnacle Officer Wilcox's private elevator. Level five."

"Received, Yarrow. Estimate time to attend monitor malfunction."

"Time to attend malfunction estimated at forty minutes. Stand by for updates."

"Proceed as logged. Standing by for updates."

Quinton clicked off his radio, running his fingers

through his neatly cropped hair. Forty minutes. Officer Cerberus would be displeased at the equipment malfunctions sustained during his shift, and more so by the delay in maintenance checks. Perhaps there was some other way to fix the monitors. The backup generators could sustain a primary level of power required for the complex. The furnaces were fueled by wood from the forest and would therefore be unaffected by the unexpected power surge. This was a comfort. Quinton did not relish the idea of spending a night without heat in his quarters.

Yet another explosion rang out. Quinton checked his timepiece. It read 20:15. This time the sound undoubtedly came from the direction of the furnaces. Officer Cerberus was right. The furnaces were a constant source of annoyance to the efficient running of the complex.

Quinton checked the power requirements of the lighting, reading eleven watts at the base of the tube. He pulled the monitor to the side, cleaning away the dust with a rag as he scanned the numbers. Eighty-five watts. A larger drain, however not so large as to be prohibitive. He checked the connection once more, unplugging it and plugging the monitor back into the power supply. The standby light for the monitor returned, showing nothing but a blank screen.

This made no sense to Quinton. The backup generator was designed to power the monitor, along with the reduced wattage lighting for the entire complex. However the standby light remained on, which theoretically meant that there was nothing wrong with the monitor.

The furnace had malfunctioned, that was all. The furnace was old, as Officer Cerberus had said, and could be unpredictable in its daily functions. It was prone to frequent explosions, and was of no concern.

A thought was playing at the back of Quinton's mind as the standby light glowed in his vision. Something about the explosions coming from the furnace, the resulting power malfunction and the monitor with its blank screen. The light glowed at him, remaining inexplicably on standby. Something was wrong. It made no sense unless...

*The explosions didn't come from the furnace.*

Quinton stood, shoulders rigid as he reached out to manually activate the Ward Beacon. He lifted the casing and swung it around to reveal the rounded button inside. Closing his eyes he pressed.

Nothing.

He pressed again, sucking in a breath. The monitor remained dormant, awaiting the signal from the beacon.

The radio crackled beside the console.

"Sound the alarm!" The panicked voice distorted in his ears.

"Bonn? Is that you?"

"...the alarm!"

"What's happening?"

"The alarm! Sound the alarm!"

"Where are you? What's happening?" He ignored the crackles, focusing on the frequency of maintenance Officer Bonn's hysterical voice.

"Alarm... elevator. Get down here!"

Quinton pushed his chair away, scrabbling for the air siren lever on the far wall. He felt along the wall, gripping the yellow handle and pushing the lever to engage. It would have to suffice, he thought, imagining the possible reprimands from Officer Cerberus. But there was no other choice. The Ward Beacon was silent, and the air siren was the only available means of alerting the facility.

The drone of the air siren blared towards the suspension zone, a warning to Internees not to attempt an escape. Few could tell the difference between the air siren and the Ward Beacon. Quinton could barely distinguish the sounds himself. He scrambled for the rear of the observation tower. As he sprinted through the walkway to the main complex, his radio crackled once more.

"Quinton! ...down here now!"

# 2

The whip of the cool breeze swirled the green and purple leaves, sending sand and loose pebbles scattering across the ground. The rocky plains were deserted, save for a boot protruding from a large rock adjacent to a circular grove of shrubs.

Beth 259201 lay propped against the rock at the site of the designated safe marker. A glint of brightness flashed in her hand as she turned something over in her palm. The regulation nail file was sharpened to a deadly point, smeared with Pinnacle Officer Wilcox's blood. Her breath huffed in her ears, echoing out of time with the beat of her heart. The siren blared faintly in the distance, rhythmically breaking the oppressive silence of the arid landscape.

201 leaned her back against the large rock, looking up to the sky. The moon was a thin sliver, surrounded by an expanse of stars that seemed to stretch on forever. 201 dropped her head back on the rock, dark hair fanning out on the stone, watching as the stars brightened and dimmed above her.

*Why am I not expired?*

The siren continued its drone, sending a shiver through her. She placed her hand over her heart, imagining the implant marker burrowed deep within her chest. The siren should have activated her implant marker, sending a charge through her heart, yet this had not happened. The rescue group must have succeeded in blowing the beacon. She rubbed at her collarbone as she scanned the area for any signs of movement, finding nothing.

*I am free.*

201 let her arms fall to her sides as a laugh welled up within her. The faint sound of the siren punctuated her laughter as the winds blew gently through the rocks and shrubs of the barren suspension zone.

*I am free.*

201 slapped the rock with her hand, pushing herself to her feet. She ran her finger over the gash in her shoulder. The seeping blood had now slowed and had begun to dry and crust at the edges. She wiped her hands, the flaking clots smearing the dark bloodstain covering the front of her blue Omega jumpsuit, now dusty and soaked with sweat. The Vassal chain clinked against her insignia as she turned in one direction, then the other, finding no sign of the rescue group she had seen so vividly in her dreams.

The rocky plains stretched out from beneath her feet in all directions. The transport and its inhabitants were gone.

# 3

High Training Officer Reno peered through the gap in the elevator doors, mesmerized by the flickering of the backup generator lights. He pushed inside, turning sideways to squeeze through the gap.

The lights buzzed and flickered over the slumped form of Pinnacle Officer Wilcox. The pooled blood glistened in the light. Spatters had started to dry near the outer edge, forming hardened flakes on the ground below. His neck was bathed in blood, the dark red liquid forming a river snaking down his side. His trouser leg had soaked up the seemingly endless pool, whereas the other side of his uniform remained mostly unblemished. Blood spatters dotted his cuffs, rivulets striping the backs of his hands. His face appeared devoid of blood, the paleness of his cleanly shaven head stark in alarming contrast to the chaos of gore spread out beneath him. Reno examined the wall behind Pinnacle Officer Wilcox's crumpled body, scanning upwards. A smattering of blood gathered around a spot on the wall, at approximately Pinnacle Officer Wilcox's height. Another set of smears gathered at arms length above the first stains, smudged from side to side. Down from these marks a large, thick smudge snaked down to the floor to mark Pinnacle Officer Wilcox's final resting spot.

A small hole in the middle of the throat peeked through the front of his pristine silver collar. Reno avoided the glazed stare of his former Pinnacle Officer, eyes methodically taking in each detail of the elevator shaft. He found a broken section of what looked like an Officer's radio in the far corner, the edges appearing splintered and jagged. The hatch at the roof of the elevator was firmly closed, a line of bloody finger marks marring the edge. A series of images filled Reno's mind, flashing in rapid succession.

An unusual weapon. Perhaps one that is easily concealed.

*Precise.*

Pierced his throat. Perhaps used the element of surprise.

*Swift.*

Held his hands above his head as he struggled.

*Strong.*

Stole a radio from a guard Officer. Broke the radio. A tactic?

*Smart.*

Reno clenched his fists. This was no accident, no last moment decision. This was a plan. A meticulous, well thought out plan.

Reno edged out of the gap between the elevator doors, nearly flattening Officer Cerberus in his haste.

"Reno."

"Officer Cerberus. I was just coming to see you."

Officer Cerberus' face was impassive, staring through the gap at Pinnacle Officer Wilcox's body.

"So. It is true."

"How did you..."

"Operator Quinton. He will not be speaking to anyone about this, I have made sure of that."

The skin on Reno's forearms went cold, prickling from the draft in the hallway. He chose not to speak. There were some times when words were not required of him, and this seemed to be one of those occasions.

"Yarrow, Bonn, they were the only other Officers aware of this... incident. They are secure for the moment. This is not of your concern, of course, all will be taken care of as of tonight. Officer Reno, I don't believe I need to explain to you the penalty for speaking of the events of this night to a fellow Officer."

"No, Sir."

Officer Cerberus continued to stare through the gap in the doors, the dim blue glow illuminating his face. Reno checked his peripheral vision. Officer Cerberus head was still, his shoulders firm, body unmoved from his position.

"Sir?"

Officer Cerberus' voice seemed to come from far away. "There is nothing to prepare us for the loss of a great leader. The mind that created such precision, such order, lost. All too soon."

Reno bowed his head.

"Rogues, I am sure of it," said Officer Cerberus.

"The shape of the wound is unusual. It was inflicted using a weapon I do not recognize," said Reno. Officer Cerberus continued to stare past him at the form of Pinnacle Officer Wilcox.

"He made the Internees safe," said Officer Cerberus. "Safe from the hordes, the mercenaries. Such a beautiful design... remove the enticement, the spoils of a female reward, remove the problem of invasion. And now this. So many processes, so much data to record, to correlate. He did most of the calculations by hand, isn't that remarkable?" Reno kept his mouth shut, unsure of what to say.

"The beauty pills, they must be maintained. And the implant markers, our stockpile is lower than I would like... and now the Ward Beacon. Catastrophe."

Reno nodded, remaining silent.

"Operator Quinton was derelict in his track and surveillance duties. A more efficient Operator would have ascertained the fact that the Ward Beacon was out." He pummeled his fist to his palm, emphasizing his words. "That is why the monitors did not power as expected. The Ward Beacon controls the monitors, and the implant marker for an escaped Internee activates the Ward Beacon. One process precedes the other. It is a seamless chain, a logical sequence. Until you get the result such as we have found here tonight. A small collection of strategically placed explosives and what happens? FERTS is defenseless. Just like that."

"How did they..."

"No implant markers, no activation of the beacon. That's how they got in. That's how they destroyed the beacon. Months of work, years of planning, obliterated. The rogues exploited our only weakness. How did they know, I wonder, how did they know?" Cerberus' eyes focused on a spot at the far wall of the elevator, the corners of his mouth tilted up in something resembling a smirk. "You know that there was an escape, some months ago, no doubt you heard."

"I heard something. A Vassal, from Beta Circuit, correct?"

"Beth 259292, 23Y. Vassal, Beta Circuit. Escaped from Vendee Yuri, township of Evergreen. I agonized for weeks over the breach of our regulations. It was my idea, my design. I put forth the idea to Pinnacle Officer Wilcox for the installation of the Township Restoration Beacon. It was my plans that were ultimately approved for installation. No Vassal will escape their Vendee in future, not from Evergreen, not from Oaklance, Lellban or Riversberg. Thanks to my design, a design for which I gained no credit."

"The Township Restoration Beacon was an important security measure," Reno said evenly.

"The Beta Internee, Beth 259292 must have known something about our systems, no doubt it was obtained from an Officer. There is no telling what an Officer will say under influence of a Vassal and cider. But still, this is unlikely. Vassals do not question. They do not learn and plan such things. There will be repercussions for any Officer who has spoken to an

Internee in this manner." He turned to Reno, smiling. "You would not breach regulations in such a manner, would you Officer Reno?"

"No, Sir," Reno replied. Officer Cerberus knew perfectly well that Reno did not care for the services of Vassals. He preferred to train the Internees, not fraternize with them.

"Nevertheless, there shall be consequences, always consequences. So much to do, so much to organize. Assemble the Officers of Zeta Circuit before morning rations. I will find out who spoke of Zeta Circuit and take appropriate action, according to regulations."

"All of Zeta, gone?"

"Every last one. It matters not, they are not high priority. They were scheduled for... ah, Reno. I forget myself. You have enough concerns in Epsilon Circuit. Your duties as High Training Officer provides a valuable service to the morale of the Officers. These matters of Zeta did not concern you in the past, and should not concern you now. The higher levels are intact. Beta, Omega, all Vassals safe and accounted for."

Reno opened his mouth to interject but thought better of it.

"I do not suspect that a Vassal could have known such things about our systems. Clearly, such a plan must have come from outside forces. These rogues were stealthy but by no means were they intelligent in their planning and execution. To procure the coveted Beta Circuit, or even Omega would have been a far more valuable bounty. Their logic is not sound. They will fetch no profits at all for their paltry collection of Zeta Internees. Foolhardy. These rogues did nothing more than provide the routine service of waste removal for the facility. Were I not so livid, perhaps I would thank them."

Reno kept his face neutral, resisting the urge to scowl. He gathered his courage to speak. "I have examined the elevator shaft. The details do not point to common mercenaries. Their methods do not fit with what I have observed."

Officer Cerberus remained silent. Reno ploughed on, undeterred. "Whoever did this, planned meticulously. It was a moment of opportunity, executed flawlessly. It is clear that a high level of intelligence was required."

"It matters not." Officer Cerberus shook his head. "None of the Internee population must know of this. The official announcement will be given tomorrow. We will let it be known that Pinnacle Officer Wilcox expired from natural processes, as is the way of things. Do you know, Officer Reno, what the consequences might be if the Internee population were informed of such a breach of our security processes? To know that a common rogue was able to expire the Pinnacle Officer himself? Chaos, Officer Reno. Chaos." Officer Cerberus squared his shoulders, clenching his jaw. "The Internee population is docile, dutiful. Their minds are fragile, as you know. We do not want any talk of such uncertainty to interfere with the order of things. That will be all, Officer Reno. Go. Investigate. Do what you must to track down these rogues. I will make preparations for the veneration of Pinnacle Officer Wilcox myself. I am the administrator of this facility, and I must continue the legacy of our great Pinnacle Officer. Now go."

"Line check!"

Officer Reno stood rigid at the railing, surveying the walkways of Omega. The line checks for Kappa, Beta and Epsilon had produced no anomalies, save for a small number of missing Internees. It was entirely possible that the week's demotions to Zeta Circuit had not yet been recorded and that some Internees were most likely in the Officers' quarters. Alongside him at the railing, the Officer's voice boomed through the span of identical doors as the Internees were checked off. Reno flexed his toes, feet remaining firm as he resisted the urge to pace.

The doors sucked open, revealing bemused Internees in varying stages of sleep and dress. One Internee scratched her eyes, another looked around blearily, attempting to smooth her tangled hair over her shoulders.

"Internees of Omega. We shall now send our gratitude to Pinnacle Officer Wilcox and FERTS, for our daily provision and protection from those who would seek to strike against our Vassals, our Fighters and our Internees."

"We send our gratitude to Pinnacle Officer Wilcox and FERTS," came the mumbled reply. One Internee attempted to return to her quarters before another Internee gripped her arm, keeping her in place.

"Internees, report as follows. 210."

"Report," came the husky reply. 210 yawned widely, covering her mouth with a delicate, manicured hand.

"219."

"Report."

"284."

"Report."

"291."

"Report."

Reno remained still, eyes scanning the line of Internees.

"276."

"Report."

*Something is wrong.*

"244."

"Report."

"261."

"Report."

"201."

Reno scanned the line of Omega Internees, the blue jumpsuits lined in regulation order, stretching on down the walkway.

"201."

The Officer's voice droned in monotone, echoing through Omega Circuit.

Reno followed the line, each Internee standing before their quarters. Each Internee evenly spaced from the next. It was only then that he spotted it. One

Internee looked to her left, scratching behind her ear as another looked to her right, revealing the gap.

"201."

"201..."

# 5

201 sat huddled on a rocky ridge, overlooking the suspension zone. There were no clear paths here, the wildness of the terrain virtually unmarked. The sand of the desert floor was littered with small shrubs and strange tangled growths that blew in the winding winds. The breeze traveled through channels, tunneling its way through towering rocks and shrubs, dislodging sand and loose leaves, paving the way forward for her journey. She shivered in the morning chill, bringing her arms around herself for warmth.

The sky was shadowed in blue, slivered tinges of pink and yellow peeking through above the few scattered clouds. 201 rubbed her arms, leaning forward to rest her elbows on her knees. She watched as the sky changed from dark blue to light. The stars faded as the sun crept into view, peeking out from behind a far mountain, washing the desert in a bright glow of orange and gold.

This was the first sunrise, the first she had seen unfold without the frame of a slivered window to hinder its brilliance. 201's breath caught as she watched the rocky desert illuminate in sections, shadows dancing across the desert floor. 201 grinned, closing her eyes to the sun as it warmed her face. She smiled until the suspension zone was revealed in garish light. Her cheeks ached, but still she smiled. It was not a practised smile, as specified in her seduction manual, nor was it a Vassal presentation smile. She felt crinkles at the corner of her eyes as she squinted into the sun. This smile was real.

201 dusted herself off and made her way down the slope of the ridge. She had trained her mind to pinpoint the trail left by the cart. She had wondered if her abilities would leave her once she was free of FERTS, that perhaps once the desire to leave her body had no longer been a necessity, she would somehow lose the ability on which she had come to rely. Instead, she felt her power growing, expanding in the morning sun, her mind clear and free from distractions. There would be no FERTS requital this morning. 201 could almost hear the drone of voices reciting the requital in unison, faces shining with adulation. She would no longer give thanks for the provision and protection of the Officers within those walls. It would be better to expire out here, where she was free, than live trapped as a dutiful Vassal within her quarters at Omega.

It was getting easier to pinpoint her awareness towards the group she had planned to join on the journey. It mattered not that she had been unable to intercept them before they left the suspension zone. They did not know of her as she knew of them and it would be difficult to explain. She would track them by following the trail, and soon enough, she would find them. She looked at her timepiece. The time read 06:03. There would be no line checks, no more regulation protein at the long tables of the ration room, no Epsilon Games, no Epsilon Chance Wheel. If she was to fight, she would be the one to choose her opponent. The Epsilon Chance Wheel would not spin for her this time. Time was hers, in abundance.

Later that night 201 lay against a tree, her mind racing. She willed her thoughts to calm down but nothing would stop the influx of images that flowed through her mind.

She saw a hand outstretched, a scroll clenched within its grasp.

*"What I ask of you is of the utmost importance,"* said the voice.

The figure nodded. He was robed, his face obscured by the hood.

*"The backup plan must be followed. It is exactly as we discussed. I want you to make sure this time. Your instructions are clear. Leave no trace."*

The voice was unfamiliar, yet the insignia on the uniform was not. The robed figure remained silent, a dark hollow where his face should have been.

*"There can be no loose threads this time."*

The hand reached out to take the scroll.

*"Destroy it. Destroy it all."*

# 6

Officer Cerberus sat at the edge of his bed, the morning too quiet, too dark to make out any of the features from his high window. He had ordered a clearing of Pinnacle Officer Wilcox's personal effects, for the purpose of veneration, he had told them. What he did not mention, and did not fully acknowledge to himself, was that he needed the reminders of the great Pinnacle Officer removed from sight. The nagging, persistent needle at the base of his neck, speaking only to him, repeating the words, the taunts, the fears he thought he had buried deep within.

*You'll never measure up.*

He knew, on some level, he knew it to be true. Reminders lay scattered all around him. There were stacks of papers, plans, designs, ideas he knew he could never envisage. The origin of these ideas came from a place, a level of thinking that he could only hope to understand. Yet, here he was. The Pinnacle Officer was gone, along with his harsh words, his derision and scorn for his loyal and efficient second-in-command. Gone now, the meetings once held in the audience of the Pinnacle Officer. The specter of

Wilcox still lingered, his presence thick within the walls.

*You cannot think this way. Wilcox is gone.*

The calculating looks, the dismissive nature of Wilcox would stay in this room, no matter how many times he called in the Officers to clean it out. He would draw on the wisdom of Pinnacle Officer Wilcox in this time of great change at FERTS. Pinnacle Officer Wilcox had taught him from the very beginning: Every Resident Citizen and Officer gained strength and single-mindedness by freeing themselves from the burden of attachment to a Vassal or worse, an common Internee. The Officers and Resident Citizens were given the chance to rise above attachment in order to create a better society, with a focus on the betterment of the individual. The Officers' needs were provided for, the Epsilon Games slaking their thirst for bloodsport and drunkenness. The Vassals and Internees provided comfort and release, an outlet for any frustrations, needs that an Officer or a Resident Citizen must satisfy in order to carry on their duties without complaint.

Some of the Officers, he noted, did not require the services of Vassals. This, he could not understand. Pinnacle Officer Wilcox had always encouraged the Officers to avail themselves of the services that Vassals were trained to provide. A Vassal studied for many years, perfecting and honing the craft of seduction. This was their designed purpose, and a fitting one, Officer Cerberus concluded. Each Internee, each potential Vassal was birthed in order to strive towards an ideal of beauty and servitude. The pleasing aspects of a Vassal always seemed to boost the morale of the Officers and fetch a higher price from the Vendees in the townships. A Vassal was to be admired, venerated. The highest complement to an Internee's efforts of grooming and seduction was to be promoted, exalted to the status of Vassal. A Vassal was held in high regard at FERTS, the title bestowing a prestige that many Internees could ever dream to achieve. Once a Vassal was actualized, the time was limited. A Vassal would be expected to perform her duties efficiently, dutifully. If a birthing occurred, and a Sire was produced, then all the better as the Forkstream Territories were in dire need of a boost to the increasingly sparse population. Many did not survive long enough to produce a Sire, and Officer Cerberus would seek to remedy this oversight on the part of his esteemed former Pinnacle Officer. He had devised his own solution to this issue, a solution that would double the resources, the profits from Vassal sales and boost the facility's defenses. It was the only way to ensure the continuation of a stable, ordered society. The only way to continue the legacy of the Pinnacle Officer.

Officer Cerberus sighed, running his hands down his pristine silver trousers. The tight singlet hugged his barrel chest, his face cleanly shaven in regulation order as specified by Pinnacle Officer Wilcox. He had bathed and shaved according to regulation, his dark hair carefully coiffed into shape. He stood, mindful of his freshly polished shoes as he made his way to the wardrobe without scuffing. The shirt and jacket peered out at him, the silver of the silk material shining as he smoothed his hand over the lapels. He dressed in silence, the lulling piped music filtering through his chambers.

*Mine, now.*

Standing before his long mirror, he surveyed the Officer he had become, his tall frame improving the look of the uniform befitting the Pinnacle Officer. He took another look at the Officer reflected back at him, the last time he would be addressed as Officer Cerberus, his last day as a simple Officer. The best day of his life was beginning.

The High Ceremonials began at first light, the Vassals assembled in the main Vassal presentation hall. The walls were a gleaming white, the FERTS logo adorning each wall. The metal lettering blended subtly with the smoothness of the walls, the white and red rounded shape abstractly representing the Vassal's birthing organs. Behind the logo were the letters XX, faintly outlined in a lighter metal. On alternating walls was the Vassal logo, the gold V encased in a ring of gold, FERTS lettering decorating the rim.

The mood was sombre, filled with expectation. Many Vassals huddled together, looking towards the podium. Officer Cerberus appeared from the shadows behind the curtains, dressed brightly in his immaculate silver uniform, full dark hair carefully coiffed, blue eyes glistening under the harsh lighting. His ruddy complexion was flushed with exaltation.

"Officers, Operators, Vassals. We shall now send our gratitude to Pinnacle Officer Wilcox and FERTS, for our daily provision and protection from those who would seek to strike against our Vassals, our Fighters and our Internees."

"We send our gratitude to Pinnacle Officer Wilcox and FERTS," came the uncertain reply.

"I am aware that many of you do not understand the reason for our gathering this morning."

Officer Cerberus took a deep breath, catching the eyes of the assembled crowd.

"Our beloved Pinnacle Officer Wilcox is expired."

A gasp rose from the crowd. A number of Vassals began to weep, their sobs echoing in the large hall.

"Pinnacle Officer Wilcox expired from natural causes. It was a departure highly fitting of the great Pinnacle Officer. He passed with a quiet reverence befitting the order and regulation we have come to enjoy as part of our privilege here, safe within the protective circle of the great organization at FERTS. Even in his last moments, Pinnacle Officer Wilcox spoke of you, dear Vassals. His thoughts were on you and your unwavering service, your dedication to the coveted role of Vassal." He gripped the lectern for effect, just as he had seen Pinnacle Officer Wilcox do in so many of his celebrated presentations.

He caught the eye of each Vassal, each Officer, acknowledging them each as in turn, just as Pinnacle Officer Wilcox had done before him. He smiled, eyes glistening, a resigned smile of one who has lost much, but must go on for the sake of many.

"You are the elite, the most gifted, the most determined, and this knowledge should make you proud, dear Vassals, not saddened. You can save your sorrow for your private veneration in your chambers while you keep the ideals clearly in your mind. Tonight, when you bathe in regulation order, pay more attention to your grooming. Study your seduction manuals, avail yourselves of the full spectrum of specially designed creams and lotions, lovingly created by Pinnacle Officer Wilcox himself. The recipes are not lost, your beauty regimen is secure. You must celebrate this knowledge, it is what Pinnacle Officer Wilcox would have wanted for you."

The Vassals composed themselves. They smiled, dabbing their eyes, returning their thoughts to venerating the great Pinnacle Officer Wilcox.

"Pinnacle Officer Wilcox was strong, but his passing was swift, and quiet. Yet nothing can prepare us for the loss of such a great leader, we must venerate him, and his legacy will continue." A smattering of applause started up in pockets of the assembled Vassals. The Officers were silent, standing to attention on either side of Officer Cerberus. The Officers were silent, standing to attention on either side of Officer Cerberus. Officer Reno stood to attention while Games Operator Farrenlowe remained stoic, dressed entirely in black.

"We must venerate the order, the precision that Pinnacle Officer Wilcox has worked tirelessly to create. Pinnacle Officer Wilcox created this..." He spread his arms wide, nodding at each of the Vassals.

"This facility, such a precise model of order, of protection, for all of you." The Vassals applauded once more. "Here you are safe from the hordes." He spat out the word. "These mercenaries. There are things you must know about them, these rogues from the Territories. There is no reason with them. They will take, and they will plunder, and there will be no mercy. No regulations, no order. Simply chaos." Another gasp rose up. Officer Cerberus' mouth twitched at the edges as he caught the eye of one of his Officers.

"The achievements of Pinnacle Officer Wilcox cannot be measured in mere words. Look around you. This is his creation. And we must venerate and continue his legacy!" The assembled crowd began to applaud, slowly at first, then gathering momentum.

"Today marks a new beginning in the legacy of this great organization. But alas, dear Vassals, we are in need of resources, scarce, as the case may be, yet not unattainable. Our needs are humble here. We do with them what we can, provide as much as we can. However we need more resources in order to keep you, our dear Vassals, safe. Safe from the hordes, the mercenaries, the untold savagery of the chaos that we keep from your delicate sensibilities. We need more resources in order to keep you protected. Safety. Security. Certainty. This is what we need. We need these to keep you provided for, to keep you in the manner that you are accustomed..." He paused for effect. The Vassals were silent, waiting for his next words.

"As a new initiative, we shall be opening the parameters of Vassal selection." A gasp rose from the crowd.

"Do not fear, dear Vassals, for your current positions are secure. Once conferred as Vassal, you are forever elevated to the standing to which you deserve, and you do deserve it, dear Vassals." A nervous giggle reverberated through the hall.

"No, this is an initiative of opportunity. The Vassal selection will now be open to those of 15Y and up. It is an inequity, a travesty indeed, that many potential Vassals are, as we speak, languishing in the drudgery of learning and grooming for far too long. Why, an Internee of 15Y is indeed ready, gifted with the attributes that are so venerated in Vassal selection. Do you wish to deprive these potential Vassals of their chance to shine? Of their chance to boost the prestige of this facility, to bring satisfaction to the growing number of potential Vendees?"

The Vassals were silent, looking to each other in confusion, unsure of what to reply.

"No!" He slapped the lectern. "No, we will not let this injustice continue! These potential Vassals must be tested immediately! Such an untapped vein of potential, going to waste. As we speak. Will you join me, Vassals? Will you encourage and guide the new Internees on their journey to Vassal selection?" An affirmative cheer rose from the assembled Vassals.

"Will you join with me in making this under-resourced facility great once more? Will you join with me, Vassals in venerating the great order and protection of FERTS?"

The enthusiastic reply came, a cheer bursting forth from the assembled Vassals.

"This is the last day we give thanks to Pinnacle Officer Wilcox. But it is the first day that FERTS becomes stronger, more secure, a paragon of control, of peace, discipline and decorum. Today is the day FERTS becomes greater than its individual components, the day FERTS becomes integrated, complete, whole. Today is the first day of a better, brighter FERTS!" The crowd erupted into a cheer, Officer Reno and Games Operator Farrenlowe joining in with the rest of the Officers in venerating the great Pinnacle Officer.

Two Officers dressed all in black, wheeled the dark, mahogany casket, adorned with silver and gold trimming, polished to a bright shine. The casket of Pinnacle Officer Wilcox.

A gasp sounded, followed by a hush of anticipation. The casket was draped in cloths of orange, red, blue and white, a heavy, burnished metal FERTS logo atop the drapery.

"We give our thanks to Pinnacle Officer Wilcox!' Chanted the Officers, the Vassals joining in, voices raised in exaltation.

"We give our thanks to Pinnacle Officer Wilcox!"

"We give our thanks to Pinnacle Officer Wilcox!"

The casket made its journey through to the back of the hall, passing Vassals on either side of the path through the assembly. Vassals wept, scrambling for a position near the passing procession, some reaching out to touch the casket, running their fingers along the silken cloths.

The casket exited through the rear doors, the doors closing, trapping the grief within.

In the silence that followed, Games Operator Farrenlowe stepped forward, spreading his arms before the crowd.

"Beloved Vassals. This is a time for celebration! I look at each of you and see the pride of FERTS. The apex of beauty, of physical perfection! And now, beloved Vassals, I ask you to give thanks, give your renewed veneration for our new Pinnacle Officer!"

"I present to you, Pinnacle Officer Cerberus!" The Vassals cheered excitedly, clapping and waving their hands towards the new Pinnacle Officer in reverence.

One of the Officers stepped forward to pin the elaborate insignia on Officer Cerberus' silver uniform as Games Operator Farrenlowe raised his hands once more.

"Esteemed Officers, dutiful Vassals. We now send our gratitude to Pinnacle Officer Cerberus and FERTS, for our daily provision and protection from those who seek to strike against our Vassals, our Fighters and our Internees."

"We send our gratitude to Pinnacle Officer Cerberus and FERTS," came the piercing cry.

Pinnacle Officer Cerberus stood, basking in the adulation, face shining with pride and exuberance. The cheers from the assembled Vassals rose through the hall, echoing throughout the deserted hallways.

# 7

201 rested in a small grove. The night was warmer, a thick blanket of cloud separating her from the night sky. The moon was half-full, a diffuse glow behind the slowly shifting clouds. The breeze was crisp, gusting to dissipate the warmth of the night. 201 ran her hands over her arms, trying to stave off the slight chill in the air. The need to move again would come soon. The nights forced 201 to keep her body moving in order to keep warm. This night provided a brief respite, but she knew the time to move would come again. She rested her elbows on her knees, blowing out a breath. There were no supplies, nothing to assist her in creating shelter or fire. The haste of her escape left no time to find the means necessary to create the one thing she required. Warmth.

201 scanned the outline of the trees against the clouds. There was no movement, no sounds to indicate that she was anything but alone in this strange landscape. She could feel the camp's inhabitants, the trail leaving remnants of their essence in the form of a thin stream of green, clear and vibrant in her mind. Her abilities had improved and she had trained herself to fix on individual figures, becoming aware of their location and the

outline of their essence. This time, the trail was vivid, the tendrils of green winding from her position to a point far off in the distance, through the rocky plains and larger rocks of the suspension zone. Her feet throbbed from the day's journey and the attempt to match speed with the camp's horse-drawn cart had proved futile. Still, she was determined to continue, following their essence until she reached her goal. This trail would lead her to safety, she was certain of it, no matter how long the journey might take.

201 slid down the rock to rest on the ground. She had not eaten for days and the gnaw in her stomach would not relent. The plan was simple. Find water, perhaps something to eat. Walk at night and rest during the day. Follow the trail. The plan focused her mind, kept it from thinking of the strangeness of the unfamiliar landscape, the hollow ache in her stomach and the chill that whipped through her jumpsuit.

201 rolled up her sleeve to check the gash on her arm. The outer edges were ragged, the redness faded to a dull pink. 201 ran her finger around the edge, feeling the uneven ridges. The flaps of skin has begun to fuse together, the exposed flesh less garish than before. 201 rolled down her sleeve, rubbing her arm for warmth. The wound was closing, that was the main concern. Her bruises had faded a little, the black and purple finger marks at her hip had paled to a greenish-yellow. 201 hissed as she pressed against the marks, her small fingertips matched against the larger grip marks left by Officer Ryan's hand. She could not check the bruises on her neck, but she supposed that

they too would fade in time. The wind picked up, rushing past her ears and weaving its way through the gaps in her jumpsuit. She shivered. The Omega jumpsuits were not designed to withstand the elements.

201 pushed herself to her feet and forced herself into a steady rhythm, crossing through forest and thick undergrowth. Something told her she should keep to the edge of the tree line, following the trail at a distance. As soon as she made her way to the edge, a bubbling, gushing noise reached her ears. The temperature had dropped slightly, cooling her cheeks. 201 rushed towards the sound, feeling the moisture in the air. She sank to her knees as the river spread out before her, the moon reflecting off the water as the surface rippled in the night air. 201 laughed, splashing her face and removing her jumpsuit to clean the wound. She immersed her shoulder in the frigid waters, gritting her teeth as the sting jolted through her body. She pulled back, dressing quickly and shaking her arm to warm herself. She looked down at her chest, the dark stain of blood dried to a crust, a vivid contrast to the blue of her Omega jumpsuit. The choice was clear, soak the jumpsuit to remove the blood or leave the stain. 201 ran her fingertips through the water, wincing as the temperature chilled her hand. The stain would have to stay.

201 made her way along the edge of the river, trailing her hand through the strange plants growing alongside the waters. She tugged experimentally at the long stalks, gripping at the furry tip. A mass of

reeds came out of the soft earth, almost toppling her. 201's eyes followed the length to the ends of the stalks, revealing a mass of thick, curved swellings, notched by ridges. 201 broke off the ends, rinsing away the mud until the water ran clear. She examined the notches, the thick orange skin and the strange hair-like coverings. She broke it into two sections, examining the white inner parts. Using her ragged fingernails, she scratched at the edge, peeling the skin away to reveal the white. Giving it a sniff, 201 took a bite, chewing carefully. The taste was strange, but not unpleasant. It was marginally better than the regulation protein she had endured in the ration room night after night. She ate another couple of pieces and drank some more water, hoping that the strange plant would not make her ill.

Warmed by the unexpected discovery of food, a tiredness began to overtake her body. She trudged back to the tree line, nestling herself under a tree. She piled the ground coverings over her body and rested her head against the crook of her good arm. 201 let her mind wander, trying to pinpoint the exact location of the camp. She wondered about the inhabitants and what she might find there once she arrived. She knew it was far from FERTS, far from any of the townships in the Forkstream Territories. A sanctuary, a place without the Circuits of Beta, Omega, Epsilon, Kappa and Zeta. A place without the need for Vassals bred for pleasure or Internees bred for fighting and hard labor. It was something she had only seen in dreams but never experienced. She listened to the beat of her heart and the sound of her breath, gently lulling her into a fitful sleep. She willed herself not to dream, however she knew she was unlikely to get her wish tonight. As she drifted to sleep, voices weaved their way through her mind, the same unfamiliar voice, the same scroll clenched in his hand.

*"Destroy it. Destroy it all."*

# 8

201 dreamed of dark hallways, the stale air a stark reminder of where she was.

"Line check!" came the voice of the Officer.

201 looked up to find the Officer smiling down at her.

"201." He leaned his elbows on the railing.

201 ignored him, continuing on down the hallway. The lights were flickering, the backup generator providing a limited source of diffuse blue light.

"Report, 201!"

201 broke into a run, making her way down the hallway. The rooms were strange, some seemed to come from Omega, some from Epsilon. All were closed. The hallways were quiet. Too quiet.

"Line check!" The voice followed her down the hallway as she headed for the ration supply unit, looking for the way out.

The ration supply unit was locked. The ration supply unit was never locked.

201 heard a barking sound, growing louder with each moment.

*The fighting creatures are out.*

201 watched a line of Vassals file through a doorway marked with an "A". They sobbed, saying

goodbye to their fellow Internees. 201 thought she caught a glimpse of Officer Reno's face as he said farewell to one of the Vassals, a little one clasped in her arms. She continued on down the hallway, searching for another exit.

"Line check, 201."

*That voice. It can't be.*

201 stiffened, her boots slipping on the stone floor.

*Don't turn around.*

"I see you, 201 and I will follow you. You can be sure of it," came the voice, that voice she would never forget, the voice of...

*Pinnacle Officer Wilcox.*

201 tucked her head down and ran, charging through the hallways, each one of them leading to a closed-off section from which there was no escape, every hallway closing in as she ran, trapping her inside.

"Forever."

201 awoke with a gasp, the faint sounds of running water trickling on the other side of the tree line. She felt tears drying on her cheeks, chilling her face.

The wind had dislodged much of the undergrowth and she shivered, clutching her midsection. She pulled her knees to her chest, the cramps squeezing at her stomach. The strange plants she had eaten had not agreed with her, yet she refused to allow her body to reject them. She gritted her teeth, waiting and breathing as the cramps tugged and pinched at her insides.

She breathed slowly, focusing her mind on thoughts of the camp, her chosen destination. This was her escape, she reminded herself, a plan of her own making. It was something she had chosen for herself, the first time she had made a conscious decision to act in her own interests, rather than deferring once more to the endless regulations and duties required of her at FERTS. She did not wish to be a Vassal, nor did she wish to be a Fighter in the Epsilon Games ring. Now her only choice lay ahead in the form of a trail, a bright green remnant, the essence of those who had presented her with her only opportunity for escape. She rested her head once more as the cramps subsided, tucking her elbow under her head. For the first time in longer than she could remember, 201 fell asleep and did not dream.

# 9

Reno stood in the door, feet spread apart, arms behind his back. Pinnacle Officer Cerberus' study was dim, the light casting shadows over the Pinnacle Officer's face. Notes, plans and calculations were spread out before him, weighted down with quartz. The Pinnacle Officer's brow furrowed as he scanned the details.

"You sent for me, Sir?"

"Reno." Pinnacle Officer Cerberus grinned, a wan, resigned expression.

Reno seated himself at the opposite end of the desk, hands clasped underneath the dark woodgrain.

"I am pleased with your progress, Reno. You have shown initiative where others have merely followed regulations. This is why I have chosen you for such an important task. Do you think you are ready for a greater responsibility? Do you believe you have shown your gratitude and loyalty in the best possible manner?"

"I do," said Reno. There was no need for him to list his achievements, his record spoke for itself.

"This is what I like about you, Reno. You are an Officer of few words." He handed over a scroll of papers, fastened with twine. "And you are an Officer of few questions. I do not need to explain the importance of this task, Reno. You will know what to do when the time comes."

Reno took the scroll and left without a word.

The next morning Reno loaded up the cart and ushered the Internees inside, flanked by two stern-faced Supervising Officers. He watched as the foremost Fighters of Epsilon clambered through the cart's cage door, notably Beth 259263, trident specialist, Beth 259278, bastard sword, Beth 259275, spatha, Beth 259277, zulfiqar, and Beth 259299, scimitar. the line of Internees, nine in all, arranged themselves in the cart, weapons secured in a holder at the front of the carriage, out of reach. The fighting creature came scrambling through the door, startling one of the four horses bridled for the journey. Reno took hold of the lead, longer than the standard lengths, and allowed the creature to sniff at the ground. Officer Tor brought one of the soiled towels from Zeta Circuit, holding it up to the creature's nose. The creature sniffed, then growled. Officer Tor stepped back, his short brown hair gleaming in the morning sun. He aimed the double pointed spear in the general direction of the creature's head to keep it at a comfortable distance.

Officer Tor formally addressed the inhabitants of the cart. "Internees of Epsilon. We will send our gratitude to Pinnacle Officer Cerberus and FERTS, for our daily provision and protection from those who would seek to strike against our Vassals, our Fighters and our Internees."

"We send our gratitude to Pinnacle Officer Cerberus and FERTS," came the enthusiastic reply.

Officer Tor settled himself next to Reno at the head of the cart and clacked the reins. The cart groaned and creaked as the horses pulled them into motion, the rhythmic clomping of their hooves matching the lilting motion of the cart.

Reno turned the cart towards the path leading from the ration supply unit. The creature caught another scent at the path, pausing to sniff at the ground until Officer Tor yanked at the lead to pull it back.

The fighting creature took off, tugging at the lead in Officer Tor's tight grip. The cart lurched to the side, turning towards the tree line, away from the route used for Vassal transportation. Reno clacked the reins in an effort to keep pace with the creature, Officer Tor tugging on the lead to slow the fighting creature's progress.

The cart reached the tree line, darting through rocks, passing shrubs and tiny pebbles that flew from the wheels as they traversed the unforgiving landscape.

The creature stopped at a large rock, sniffing around the base, sharp, beady eyes darting around the rocky plains of the suspension zone. The creature paused, its muscled flanks twitching, a low growl welling in its throat. Reno motioned for Officer Tor to stop just as the creature scurried forward, leading the cart through a steep winding path, barely wide enough for the cart to comfortably fit. The horses skittered on their hooves, fighting against the weight of the cart and its passengers.

"You need to get out and walk," said Reno. "Take the three supply bags, follow the creature, it will take some weight off the horses."

Officer Tor stepped from the helm, darting out of range of the cart and charging down the path to keep pace with the creature.

Reno pulled back on the reins, easing the horses through the next turn. They reached the bottom with an uneven jolt, the cart righting itself clumsily as Reno halted the horses. He turned to check on the Internees. All remained within their seats, arms casually looped around the wooden bars of the cage. Officer Tor edged towards the cart, dragging the uncooperative creature behind him, his hand grasping the double pointed spear.

"Wait!" Reno hopped down from the cart, scanning the sandy ground. The sand bore no track marks, no wheel marks, nothing to indicate that others had been through this patch of the suspension zone. Yet his eyes were drawn to the sand, struggling to make sense of the swirling patterns, the distinct yet unnatural evenness of the desert floor. He bent to inspect the markings, following the scratches and circular branding with his fingers.

"Wait here," he instructed Officer Tor. Reno made his way over to a small purple-tinged shrub, its foliage thick and tightly packed. Plucking a branch from the bush, he proceeded to sweep, first side to side, then swirling in a figure eight pattern. He looked to the original markings, satisfied that they were comparable to his own.

"They covered their tracks," he called out.

He turned to the fighting creature, watching it pace, sniffing the trail. The edges of Reno's mouth twitched. Sweeping the tracks would not dislodge the scent trail, and fighting creatures were excellent trackers, given the opportunity.

Officer Tor rejoined him at the helm, letting out carefully measured lengths of leather for the fighting creature to continue its search. The creature sniffed, following an unseen line around a winding path opening out to a small grove. The cart followed noisily behind, wheels scraping on sand, stuttering as the sand gave way to a rocky, pebbled surface.

The creature paused at a flat rock, sniffing around the edge before taking off down one of the myriad of sprawling paths into the hilly terrain, winding through the maze of rocks and valleys.

The cart trundled forward, the horses trotting feverishly as they passed more purple and green shrubs, large rocks and small hillocks. Before long they reached a collection of towering boulders. The creature stopped, sniffing at the ground before whimpering against a large, flat rock. Reno alighted from the cart, checking the rock for signs of activity, finding nothing out of place at first. It was then that his eye caught the lip of the rock, a tiny stain peeking out at him. Reno peered closer at the stain, eyes narrowing.

It was a single drop of dried blood.

# 10

201 awoke to the full heat of the day bearing down on her. A mass of birds screeched, flying up from the trees, casting shadows across her face. The ground was warm in the spot where her body had compressed the undergrowth and her body was stiff from the uncomfortable sleeping position.

She made her way down to the river, washing her face and gathering up a small collection of the strange plants to take with her on her journey. No matter how much they had disagreed with her, they would suffice as a food source, and she had no indication of where or when more food would be available in such a plentiful supply. As she snapped off the ends of the plants, a thought gnawed at her, an idea hidden in the recesses of her mind. The air was still and no sounds reached her ears. Despite this, something felt wrong. She sensed a growing urgency to get moving as quickly as possible. 201 washed the plants and packed them in her pockets, breaking into a slow jog, following the essence of the cart and its inhabitants.

201 followed a clearing in the trees. She turned, doubling back and making her way to the top of the mountain, the layers of undergrowth crunching

beneath her feet. She stopped, eyes tracking her surroundings.

*This is wrong. This is all wrong.*

A chill ran through 201 as she neared the top. Something told her to run, to turn around and retreat, but she had to know. It was only when she reached the ridge that she understood. She dropped, falling to her knees and inching forward to peer over a rock at the edge.

A cart pulled by horses was slowly making its way through the woodlands, following the very path she had taken earlier that morning. She could not make out the figures at the helm, though she felt a familiarity as she stared down at them. The cart was large, with wooden bars encasing the carriage. Within the cage 201 could see a mass of red, the red she had worn every day as she trained under the instruction of High Training Officer Reno to become a Fighter.

The red of Epsilon.

A shrill bark rang out through the valley, carrying through the expanse of space until it reached her position. 201 squinted, trying to focus on the tiny figures below. It didn't matter, none of it mattered now. She knew that sound. The sharp, snapping bark, followed by a rumbling growl, the barks and growls alternating until they seemed to merge into one. It was familiar. As familiar as the airless heat of the Epsilon Games ring, the metallic tang of blood in the air, the rustle of sawdust shavings beneath leather boots and the clink of metal against metal.

That sound could only have come from a fighting creature.

You have to relax, 201, she told herself. It's not you they're after. They search for Zeta Circuit and the ones that took them.

A smaller, more insistent voice rose up within her.

*Are you sure?*

# 11

Reno pulled on the reins, slowing the horses to a stop. The horses needed to drink and their spot close to the river would be ideal for setting up camp for the night. Reno checked the ration bags, removing the pieces of dried regulation protein for the Epsilon Fighters. He and Officer Tor would avail themselves of the more appetizing rations of dried meats and fruit.

The fighting creature grew anxious, sniffing around the edge of the tree line. Officer Tor called out to the creature, slowly pulling it back so it could be secured. He tied the lead around a large stone and went about gathering supplies for the night.

Reno scratched a small amount of flint on a dried pile of moss.

"We need more kindling, Officer Tor."

Officer Tor foraged at the tree line, collecting dried twigs and tucking them under his arm. Reno held out his hand, grabbing the sticks to build up the fire. The twigs caught, releasing a fragrant smoke.

"Do you think we'll find them?" asked Officer Tor, handing Reno another bundle of sticks. "Do you believe we will gain the adulation of our new Pinnacle Officer for our service to FERTS?"

Reno shrugged, staring at the flames flicking out between the wisps of smoke.

"The fighting creatures are good trackers, when and if they behave. I believe we will find them."

"I have never had the opportunity to deal with mercenaries. Have you?"

"No." Reno poked at the fire, stacking more wood on the layers of kindling. He looked up to find Officer Tor still watching him.

Reno returned his gaze to the fire as it took hold, crackling to life. "I once saw a group. A long time ago. I was too small to fight them so I was forced to hide." He waved a hand, dismissing the thought. "It is not a pleasant memory."

"I was told when I was very small that Pinnacle Officer Wilcox created peace where before there was nothing but war. Now I fear that something is not right, now that he is gone."

"Pinnacle Officer Wilcox created order. It was the only way to deal with the threat of mercenaries," said Reno.

"But why do we seek them now?" Officer Tor asked, his brow furrowed in concentration. "I thought that the Pinnacle Officer had guaranteed the Internees protection from mercenary attacks."

"Too many questions, Officer Tor. It's not our place to ask questions and you know the penalty for speaking of this to your fellow Officers. Go and secure the horses for the night, they've had all the water they can carry."

"Yes, Sir."

Officer Tor made his way to the horses, leading them one by one to a grove of trees, securing the reins to the branches.

The fighting creature sat on its haunches, sniffing the air and emitting a low growl. Its eyes glinted in the half-light of the early evening. It had been restless all day, but now it had become agitated. This sudden change in behavior had not escaped the attention of Reno or Officer Tor.

"It smells something, doesn't it?" said Officer Tor, watching as the creature twitched, rearing up from its hind legs and scampering forward, only to be jerked back by the lead. It let forth a high pitched whine, scrabbling at the dirt and grunting, attempting to shrug off the lead. The lead pinched against its throat, bunching the skin around its neck as its legs stretched uselessly in the air, grappling at nothing before coming to rest on the ground. The creature lurched itself once more in the direction of the path along the river, its growls compressing in a hoarse yelp as the leash pulled taut.

"We're close. The creature has caught scent of something," said Officer Tor, dropping another load of wood at Reno's feet. "We must be close or it wouldn't be acting like that."

Reno stoked the fire. "Yes, I suppose we are," he said, nodding as Officer Tor returned to the tree line to collect more wood.

"But to what?" he muttered to himself, watching the flames dance and flicker.

# 12

201 trudged along the moonlit ground, placing one foot in front of the other. She now had to keep moving in order to stay ahead of one cart and follow the trail of another. It was clear she could not outrun the horses of the Epsilon cart, at least not for any significant length of time. The bulk of the day had been spent walking at a steady pace, but now her plans required modification. If she walked too quickly through the night, she would tire and need to rest. If she rested for too long, the consequences would be equally devastating.

She headed away from her chosen path, putting distance between herself and the last known position of the Epsilon cart. This new route would no doubt hinder her efforts in finding the location of the camp, but she could not risk revealing the location of the camp to outside forces, especially those from FERTS.

201 brushed against thickly grouped branches, the sharp points pricking at her skin. She caught a glimpse of her shoulder, now covered in scratches and bleeding from the edges of the wound.

She pondered the appearance of the Epsilon cart. How did the Officers expect to find the rescue party when she herself had found it difficult to follow the remnants of their essence? Perhaps she was not the only one who could see as she did. But such an idea made no sense. Another with her abilities would have been sent to Zeta as a defective. No, they must have employed a different method.

*Why did they bring a fighting creature?*

201 knew nothing of fighting creatures save from what she had seen in the Epsilon Games ring. They were ferocious in battle, that much was clear, though she could not understand why Reno would take one of these creatures on such a journey.

201 reached a grove of trees and came to a stop, doubling over and panting for breath. She was in need of water. Food was a lesser concern at this time. She had gone for many nights with half rations or less in order to reduce muscle mass for Vassal selection. The search for food could wait.

She changed direction, making her way back to the sound of running water. She would need more water if she planned to divert from the river's path for any length of time.

201 glanced around, checking the area for any signs of movement but the river's edge was clear of activity.

She moved forward, snapping the timepiece from her wrist, tucking it away in her pocket and bending to drink from the water's edge. The water was chilling, cooling her throat as she drank as much as she could manage without coughing.

201 raised her head from the water. A tingle started on the back of her neck, whisper-soft touches

spreading down to her shoulder blades, fanning outwards.

A low growl rumbled behind her. A clicking, purring sound started up, a constant stream of sound that raised the hair on her arms.

201 turned her head slowly to find the fighting creature staring at her, eyes beady in the moonlight, the light glinting off its fur. Its hindquarters twitched, leg darting out to the side.

201 turned her body in a slow arc, bending upwards from the waist, hands raised in placation. She faced the creature, keeping her face neutral.

"Do not be afraid, I won't hurt you," she said, keeping her palms facing outwards. The creature followed her movements with its eyes.

Its fur was dark with a white line striped on its forehead. The small pointed ears jutted out to the side, dwarfed against its large rounded skull and protruding jowls. The creature's body was all compact muscle, its limbs forever bent in Fighter pose. Its eyes seemed to be set too small in its head. They peeked out, a flat gold that appeared to be lit from within, but that was just a trick of the moonlight, 201 was certain of this. It appeared to be smiling at her, its ragged fangs flashing in and out of its mouth as it growled its steady rhythm. She tried to tune into the creature's essence. Softening her gaze, she saw the creature bathed in an orange light. She sensed an alertness, a readiness to fight. She opened her mind, going deeper. The creature radiated instinct, a strange, arcane set of behaviors. 201 tried once more to connect on some level with the creature's essence. She found only questions within, and an elemental fire that sparked and burned in random patterns, an essence that was incapable of compromise or reasoning.

201's stomach clenched as a chill ran through her. The creature remained poised, motionless.

201 bent slowly to the ground, keeping her head raised, maintaining eye contact. The creature let out a bark followed by a growl, flashing its unnaturally sharpened teeth.

*They sharpen their teeth to make the fights more interesting. Quicker. Bloodier.*

201 felt at the ground until she found a large stick. Standing once more, she did not let the creature out of her field of vision.

Something was nagging at her, taunting her from the back of her mind.

I am doing something wrong, she thought. I don't know what it is but I know this to be true.

"It's okay," she said, keeping her voice soft and soothing. "I am not here to hurt you." She hoped that on some level, the creature understood. That perhaps the signals she was sending would somehow reach their mark.

It remained still, standing guard against her only escape route, the muscles on its back twitching, feet restless, shuffling at the ground. Its claws dug into the dirt.

201 tensed. Something had changed in the creature's demeanor, but she could not pinpoint the

reason for this. She stared at the creature and the creature stared back, eyes boring into her, revealing nothing of what lay beneath its mask. There was something about its eyes, something she had missed, something she should have known but had failed to recognize.

Something fundamental about...

*Its eyes.*

A coldness enveloped her, starting as a sliver at the base of her spine. It slid through her body, coiling upwards, making its way to the back of her neck. There was something about the creature's eyes, something about the way it seemed to see through her defenses, staring a challenge, a challenge, a challenge...

*Its eyes! You're looking at its eyes! Stop looking at its eyes!*

Its eyes glinted, widening to reveal the whites, then narrowing.

It let forth a whine as it bent and leapt.

# 13

Reno did not understand why he was awake. The sounds of running water at the edge of the river filtered through his awareness. He blinked, rising on one elbow. There seemed to be no immediate danger in the vicinity. He took a glance at the cart, set back from both the river and the fire. The Epsilon Fighters appeared to be sleeping, with nothing seeming out of place at first glance.

He pulled himself up to a seated position, rubbing his eyes. The embers of the fire glowed and flickered, the light around him dull and diffuse. He listened for any sounds of approaching danger and heard nothing. Yet he had woken during the night, something that rarely happened. There must have been a reason, but it was not clear what that reason might have been. A chill rippled through his body, despite the relative mildness of the night air. He looked over to see Officer Tor upright, awake and staring in his direction.

"Why are you awake?" Reno asked.

"I'm not sure, I have a strange feeling," said Officer Tor. "Nothing seems out of place. I hear nothing..."

A rumbling bark sounded out, followed by a growl. The sounds came from somewhere farther up river. Reno glanced over at the fighting creature's usual resting spot to find the tattered remains of the leash wound around the rock.

He sprang to his feet, arming himself with a spatha. Officer Tor followed, carrying a double pointed spear and a bundle of leather. Reno led the way, following the sound of the fighting creature. The growls and hoarse barks sounded pained, agitated.

The fighting creature was attacking.

Reno and Officer Tor charged through the overgrown path next to the river, the growls of the fighting creature echoing through the surroundings. Reno heard small creatures scurrying in the undergrowth, rustling through the tree line, heading for safety.

"Are you ready?" he called over his shoulder.

Officer Tor called out an affirmative, rushing to catch the pace of Reno's stride.

The commotion up ahead sounded frenzied, out of control. Reno hoped that whatever it was they were running towards, they weren't going to be too late.

# 14

The fighting creature leapt into the air, jaws stretched wide, aiming for 201's throat.

201 felt time slow down. She saw the point of the creature's sharpened teeth, the paws thick and long, delicate, reminding 201 of fingers, pink nails poking out from beneath the soft fur. But most of all she saw the creature's eyes, flat, lifeless, the eyes unflinching as they stared back at her own.

She watched the creature's soft underbelly rise alongside her as she ducked out of the way, jabbing her stick sideways into the creature's exposed midsection. She rolled, dimly aware of the splash as the creature sailed past its mark and landed in the river. There was a moment of silence as the creature was submerged.

When the creature surfaced, the barks grew wild, unbidden, chilling the hairs at the base of her spine. She sprinted, charging towards the tree line, hearing the scrabbling of the creature at the muddied earth at the water's edge. She leapt for the first tree with low hanging branches, launching herself at the lowest branch and hooking her arms and legs around it. She peered down, watching the creature haul itself from the river, shaking its hindquarters and launching its body towards her. She jabbed the stick down, hitting the creature in the forehead. It yelped, backing off and growling with renewed vigor. Its eyes grew wilder, its gaze boring into her own as it lunged again. 201 shivered, sensing the pure fear and instinct dwelling within the depths of those eyes.

The creature leapt, hitting its shoulder against the tree. It backed up and leapt again, falling short of its mark by less than a foot of distance. 201 jabbed with the stick, keeping the creature from reaching the required height to topple her from the branch.

201 watched in fascination as the creature unleashed its rage against the tree, biting at the bark and scrabbling with its claws. Its mouth came away bloody, trickles running from the corners, mixed with drool and sweat.

"Break!" yelled a voice from the edge of the tree line, the sound carrying from the side nearest to the river. "Break! Stand down!"

The creature paused, its eyes clearing to reveal awareness of its surroundings. The sound of the voice, or perhaps the word, had stopped the creature, leaving it panting on its haunches, awaiting instruction. Perhaps it had merely recognized the futility inherent in its attack.

It looked up, its brow furrowing as Officer Reno crashed through the undergrowth, another Officer leashing the creature, pointing the double pointed spear at its face when the creature resisted with a growl. The growling tapered off, leaving only the rapid panting of the fighting creature. Exhausted, it collapsed on its forelegs, resting its chin and huffing, a thin stream of drool escaping from its mouth.

"You up there. Come down."

201 scanned her surroundings, checking for an alternative route. She could climb to the top of the tree, but that would only prolong the inevitable. She could try to run, but the sight of the creature at the Officer's feet was enough to stop that particular line of thought. She scrabbled at the branch, losing her footing as she tried to descend, landing in a heap at Officer Reno's feet.

Officer Reno scowled down at her. 201 took in his familiar black uniform, complete with leather armour detail. He stood rigid, as always, his broad shoulders straight, head neatly shaved.

"Hello, 201."

# 15

"Reno, it is... good to see you," said 201, her heart thumping in her chest. She looked over at the fighting creature, catching its half-lidded gaze. It let forth an apathetic growl, huffing and resting back on its paws.

"I want that fighting creature secured at all times, Officer Tor!" Reno called out, his eyes never leaving 201.

"Yes, Sir."

Officer Tor started off towards the river, dragging the uncooperative creature behind him. The fighting creature had decided it was time to sleep, and Officer Tor found the lead becoming heavier with each step. He persisted, yanking the lead every few steps, pointing the double pointed spear at the creature to keep its jaws away from his legs. Reno gestured with his spatha, pointing it at 201's back, leading her towards the river.

"201, I would like to know what you are doing out here, without the supervision of a Vassal cart and so far from any of the townships," he said, giving her a prod with the spatha to keep her moving. She winced, feeling the coolness of the unsheathed blade against her jumpsuit.

201 remained silent.

Reno stepped in front of 201 to face her, taking in her appearance with a scowl. He reached out to her shoulder, pulling at the fabric of her jumpsuit. "You're hurt."

"A little," muttered 201. She edged past him, walking ahead, glancing at the surroundings from the corner of her eye, looking for a way to escape. Between the river and the wooded areas, the choices did not look promising. The fighting creature growled, followed by a shout from Officer Tor. They were too close. Too close to run. It would have to wait, for now.

"Stop, 201." Reno stepped before her once again, gesturing to the front of her jumpsuit. "This is more than a little."

"Not my blood." 201 resumed walking, only to be stopped again by an elbow to her windpipe. Her vision blurred for a moment before she found herself on her knees, the coolness of Reno's spatha resting underneath her chin.

"Give me one good reason why I do not expire you right now," said Reno.

So, this is it. All of this just to be expired by your former Training Officer. Is this how it ends, now? Do not expire me, Reno. Not now. Not when I was so close.

201 coughed, choking on a breath. She sucked in another breath to calm herself, attempting to sound unaffected.

"You will not expire me, Reno. You wish to ask me questions." 201 stared up at him, jaw clenched firm as she stifled another cough.

"Or perhaps the fighting creature will help you find your voice?"

201's eyes widened. "No! I do not wish... I ask you not to bring that creature near me again."

"Then talk!" Reno shouted.

His brow was sweaty, 201 noticed. Drops of perspiration ran from his temples, sliding down past his ears. Reno's squinted down at her, his face contorted in a grimace. He leaned closer to her. "You place me in a difficult position, 201. Do not think that I will not expire you if that is what is required of me." He shifted closer again, pointing the tip of the spatha's blade against her throat.

"Explain yourself, 201. I will not ask again."

201 took a deep breath. Her mind raced, the thoughts running faster and faster until it was difficult to keep track. She kept her breathing steady, attempting to slow the beating of her heart. She turned her eyes to meet his.

"They took me."

Think faster, 201, she said to herself, her mind jumping ahead to find the words she required. She felt the itch of the cold metal pressed against her throat. 201 sucked in a breath, trying to direct her gaze between Reno's eyebrows to avoid his stare.

"The mercenaries took me. From the halls." She breathed out a shaky breath, looking down at the ground.

"Why you? Why not the other Vassals?" He nudged the spatha, tilting her face upwards. "Why only Zeta Circuit?" He gritted his teeth. "Why did they do what they did?" he shouted, spittle flying in her face.

"I don't know. They did not say." 201 trained her eyes at the ground once more.

"And this?" He gestured to her jumpsuit and the dull brown stain covering her torso.

201 felt Reno's eyes on her, calculating. She cleared her throat. "I expired one of them. He will not be trying that again." She felt the beginnings of a smile and forced herself to suppress it, steeling her face into a blank mask.

Reno glanced around at the deserted surroundings, turning back to her. "And where is this mercenary now?" His voice rose in intensity. "This expired mercenary you speak of?" He stood back, arms outstretched. "I see nobody here! Where are they all now, 201?"

"They took him away with them. On horseback."

"So, what you are telling me is that you were taken from FERTS, by mercenaries."

"Yes." 201 nodded, head bowed.

"And these mercenaries, you managed to expire one of them, even though you are not a trained Epsilon Fighter, then you somehow avoided the retributions of the others. By stealth, perhaps?"

201 nodded again.

"So you were able to see them take this mercenary on horseback, yet they did not find you."

"That is correct," said 201. "I hid to stay out of sight. They were not aware of my presence."

"And now you are..." Reno looked around the wooded area, glancing back to the river. He turned back to her, exasperated.

"Lost. I am lost. At least I was, until now." She attempted a smile, hoping it looked more convincing than it felt.

Reno narrowed his eyes. 201 could feel his mind considering his choice between two options. His brow furrowed, the two opposing ideas warring for dominance.

201 moved her hands up to smooth her hair, brushing down her jumpsuit and checking her nails. She tried to check her mannerisms, attempting a presentation smile.

Reno looked down at her, a smirk forming at the corner of his mouth. "Well then, 201. I underestimated you. Perhaps not for the first time. FERTS will be proud of you and your service to the defense and protection of the Vassals."

201 hissed out a breath. She trained her gaze at the ground, processing his words.

"Thank you," she muttered, pushing herself to her feet. She attempted to move ahead, but Reno's hand gripped her arm.

"Do not think this is the end of my questioning, 201. There is something you are not telling me, and I will find out what it is, no matter how long it takes. I am patient, as you know."

"Yes. I know." 201 kept her eyes to the ground, walking ahead with Reno's spatha poking at her back.

*And so am I.*

They walked in silence for a few moments before Reno spoke again.

"Did any from Zeta Circuit escape, as you did?"

"No, not that I saw."

"So you saw them?"

"I did not say that." 201 turned to face him. "I have never seen one from Zeta Circuit." She held his gaze, the truth reverberating between them.

"I believe you, 201. But there is something you are not telling me."

"What makes you so sure?" she asked him.

Reno studied her face. "There is something about you that is different. Something about your eyes. Something has changed since the time I last trained you in Epsilon Circuit."

201 stared into his eyes. "The last time you saw me, Reno, I had not expired another. It changes you. Surely you know that."

"How? How does it change you exactly?"

"I don't know. But there is something within me, something that will never be the same. My hands have taken another. No matter who they were and what they did, they are not the one left. They are not the one who must face what they have done."

"This perplexes me, 201," he said, adjusting his grip on the spatha.

"I do not see why it would surprise you. You see it every month in the Epsilon Games."

"The rest of the Epsilon Fighters do not speak as you do," said Reno.

201 smiled at him. "Well, I am not an Epsilon Fighter, as you said."

"No, you are a Vassal." He looked her over, taking in her matted brown hair, dry olive skin and hazel eyes framed by puffy skin tinged a dark blue. "Apparently."

201 remained silent as they came upon the makeshift camp. The cart, filled with Epsilon Fighters, was devoid of activity. She spotted a mass of red hair in the corner of the cart.

201 tensed. "Reno. Do not put me with them."

"You are an Internee, 201, whether you are Omega or Epsilon, and you will stay with the other Internees in the cart. Unless you prefer to sleep with the fighting creature?"

201 shook her head.

Reno pushed her forward with the spatha, unlocking the cage. 201 watched the key click inside the lock, eyes tracking the movement as Reno returned it to his pocket.

"Get in."

201 entered the cart. A mass of red hair stirred in the far corner. Beth 259299 leaned up on one elbow, studying 201. She smiled, baring white teeth and narrowing her eyes. 201 clenched her fists, attempting to move past her.

"201. I know you." She looked at 201, eyes dragging over her form. "Hm. You don't look like a Vassal to me. I thought Vassals were supposed to be... pretty? You look like you've just rolled in mud. You look awful, in fact. You are in need of a regulation bathing as well. You stink."

201 kept her mouth shut, wedging herself in a bare section of the wooden cart. She stared through the bars, trying to tune out the sound of 299's voice. 299 leaned forward, studying 201's face.

"Yes. I know you, Vassal." 299 grinned at her. "Oh, yes... and I remember your companion, 232." 299 yawned, resting back and tucking her hair behind an ear. "I enjoyed expiring her."

201 turned her head, locking eyes with 299. 299 smiled, raising an eyebrow.

201 squeezed her eyes shut, the smiling face of 232 rising in her vision. She thought of 232's freckles, the hope in her blue eyes. She remembered 299's scimitar, flicking and swirling, the smile on 299's face. She cried out, launching herself at 299. She landed blows on 299's face, her cheeks and her eye before 299 kicked her off, hitting her knuckle against 201's temple.

201 stared up at her, head throbbing, her mind focusing on the nail file tucked within her boot.

No, she told herself. They will know it was you.

299 laughed, her voice reverberating throughout the cage. "I like you, 201. You have no chance against me, yet you tried. But it seems your bravery does not match your abilities."

201 glared at her.

"What's the matter, whelp? Lost your will to fight? Now I am awake, I would be pleased to fight you." 299 prodded at her shoulder, making 201 wince.

"Save it for the Epsilon Games, 299," Reno called from his position by the fire.

"No, I do not wish to fight you." 201 leaned her back against the bars of the cart, rubbing idly at her temple.

"Hm," said 299. "A pity. Still, we have time, whelp. Or should I call you Vassal? Are you Vassal or Fighter? You do not behave like a Vassal, that is clear. Perhaps you are confused." 299 tugged at the Vassal chain around 201's neck, running the metal over her fingers.

"Quiet," muttered a voice from further down the cart. "We are trying to sleep."

299 lowered her voice, eyes trained on 201's arm. "Ah, but now you have this." She ran her finger along the gash in 201's jumpsuit. "Yes, this will leave a scar, what a pity. I suppose you will no longer be a Vassal after all. It seems your choices are narrowing. Perhaps you will indeed come back to us at Epsilon." She narrowed her eyes at 201. "If so, I very much look forward to fighting you. I am sure my fellow Fighters will feel the same. We just love fresh meat."

201 stared back at 299 from her corner of the cart. Something in her eyes made 299 flinch. 299 composed herself once more, smiling at 201.

201 did not break the stare.

"Enjoy your sleep," said 201, a smile playing at her lips.

299 blinked, chuckling to herself and flipping on to her back. 201 watched as her breaths evened out, rumbling into a snore.

She watched the embers of the fire glowing, listening to the sounds of running water, the strange sounds emanating from the grove of trees to her right. She glanced over at the fighting creature, its eyes closed for now, the muscles on its back smoothed out. She alternated between watching the fighting creature and the sleeping figure of 299 until her eyes refused to stay open. A night bird screeched, crying out far in the distance as sleep closed in around her. As she drifted towards sleep, she was certain she could hear the sound of Pinnacle Officer Wilcox's laughter.

# 16

201 dreamed of a forest, bright green foliage trailing on her face as the sun shone through the leaves. She wandered, breathing the faint hint of wood smoke, listening to the sounds of laughter rising up to meet her. A bird cried, its blue and purple wings fluttering as it soared towards the sky.

201 watched, hand raised above her head as the bird left the canopy of the forest.

She stopped, her feet skittering on crumbling stone. Digging her heels into the ground, she watched as pebbles flew over the edge of a cliff, cascading down as her stomach dropped away. She lurched back, gripping a branch from a nearby tree.

The forest ended, abruptly dropping to nothing over the jagged cliffs. The patterns on the stone radiated out in waves, layers, the textures and shades standing out against the green of the forest.

The pebbles flew towards the ground, bouncing, changing direction.

*Tink!*

*Tink!*

*Tink!*

The pebbles landed at the feet of a little one. She wore no insignia, but she could not have been more than 10Y. She wore a simple brown tunic and cloth pants. Her feet were covered in leather, coarse seams dotting the edges of her hand-made shoes.

She bent down to pick up a pebble, looking up to meet 201's eyes.

"Hello," she said. "What is your name?"

201 looked down at her. "I am Beth 259201."

"Oh."

"You can call me 201."

"201. That's a funny name." The little one giggled, the sound echoing off the cliffs to reach 201's ears.

"What is your name? Is this... what is this place?"

"This is my home."

"Home?"

"Where I live. Don't you have a home? Where do you live?"

201 struggled with her answer. It seemed to her to be two different questions.

"I know where you live, 201." The little one's voice changed. She no longer had the voice of a little one. The voice was not one but many. Deeper, croakier, more like...

"Yes, I know you, 201," the voices said. "I will know you by your stain, your scar, the remains and the reminders of what you did to me. I will follow you until you are senseless, then I will speak while you sleep, feed you my thoughts until you can think no more. You will never be alone now that you have me."

*Wilcox.*

"Yes, 201, Wilcox. Pinnacle Officer Wilcox. The one and only Pinnacle Officer, do not be fooled by others. They will never understand my vision." The voices raised, not merely a few voices, but hundreds. "All I created is lost, all because of a defective! An ineffective Vassal and a failed Fighter!"

201 stood firm, her left hand beginning to shake. She clenched it, stifling the movement.

"Why... why do you have many voices?"

The voice was silent.

"Answer me!" 201 yelled.

"Strays. Refuse. They... follow me."

"I don't understand."

"It matters not, 201." His voice became that of the Pinnacle Officer once more. The sound was flat, uninflected. "I am glad you are back where you belong. When you return to FERTS you will be sent to Zeta and I shall personally watch as you burn along with the others. It will be a great triumph."

201 felt a prickling on her skin. The forest was alight, sparks flying around her. Her skin burned, flesh igniting from the inside, her hair, eyes, her fingernails, all on fire, the pain so intense that 201 wished she could be expired rather than feel what she could feel now.

201 clenched her teeth, refusing to scream.

# 17

201 awoke to the sound of voices. For a moment she forgot where she was but the wooden bars provided an unwelcome reminder. Reno brushed past the cage, loading up some wood in the front of the cart.

Officer Tor tapped the wooden bars with his double pointed spear, rousing the Epsilon Fighters around her.

"Fighters of Epsilon. We are gathered to send our gratitude to Pinnacle Officer Cerberus and FERTS, for our provision and protection against those who would strike against our Vassals, our Fighters and our Internees."

"We send our gratitude to Pinnacle Officer Cerberus and FERTS," came the sleepy reply from the Epsilon Fighters around her. 201 kept her mouth shut, refusing to join in the requital.

"Who is Cerberus?" 201 turned to Beth 259263.

"Oh, you didn't know," said 263, her face tight with tension. She scratched at her blonde hair, still matted from sleep. "Pinnacle Officer Wilcox is... he is expired."

"How?" 201 dug her fingernails into her palm.

"It was natural. A peaceful end for the great Pinnacle Officer. We must venerate him."

"I see," said 201.

"They say Pinnacle Officer Cerberus was the highest ranking Officer at FERTS. You would know this if you were not found wandering around here... and what was it you were doing out here exactly?"

"I have told Reno everything. I do not wish to speak of it again."

"And you spoke to Reno as to why your jumpsuit is covered in blood?" 263 reached out, pulling at the material.

201 batted her hand away. "Yes, and I do not wish to speak of it." Her voice was flat, devoid of emotion.

263 shrugged, rubbing the sleep from her eyes. "Well, what do you think? Do you think we will find the mercenaries?"

201 glanced over at the hindquarters of the fighting creature as it drank from the lake. Officer Tor stood guard behind the creature, grappling to hold both lead and double pointed spear.

It found *me*.

"With that creature? Yes, it is likely we will find something." 201 held still, suppressing the chill that ran through her body.

"You do not seem very excited about the prospect. I look forward to defending the honor of FERTS. We cannot allow mercenaries to strike against our Vassals, our Fighters or our Internees, even if they are from Zeta Circuit."

201 stiffened. "What do you mean, even if they are from Zeta Circuit?"

"Why would you ask such a thing? Everybody is aware that Zeta Circuit is for the lame, the useless, the defective. You know this as well as I do, 201."

"You could be sent to Zeta Circuit, just as easily as I could. You know this as well, 263."

263 turned to face her. "No, 201. I do not believe that to be true. Nobody is sent to Zeta without good reason, and besides, that is a matter for the Officers to decide in their wisdom. Anyway, you are far more likely to be sent to Zeta Circuit. It seems you are becoming known for your refusal to follow regulation." She glanced sideways at the figure of Officer Reno approaching the cart.

Reno made his way over to the lock to open the cage, allowing a couple more of the Epsilon Fighters outside to stand and stretch their legs.

"I look forward to it! Maybe I will see you there, 263!" 201 yelled through the bars. She leaned back against the back of the cart, laughing, her eyes vacant. She kicked against one of the bars before getting a reproachful look from Officer Reno.

"Why must they place us in the cart with this Omega Internee?" 263 muttered to herself, shaking her head at 201, now locked alone in the cage.

Beth 259275 joined her, lowering her voice to a whisper. She flicked her black hair over her shoulder. "Did you know that she tried to fight 299 last night? She is truly lucky that 299 did not take her up on the offer."

"Yes, I heard," said 263.

"What was she doing out here?" asked 275.

"I do not know. Officer Reno is aware of her situation. I presume he will deal with 201 according to regulations. It is not our place to question such things."

"No, it is not our place," said 275.

"I fear she is dangerous," 263 said.

275 glanced back at the cage, watching 201 pace the length of the cart, muttering to herself. She flopped down in the corner, giving the bars another kick.

"She does not look so dangerous to me," said 275. "Look how frail she is. She has barely any muscle mass to speak of. I could probably fight her without my chosen weapon."

263 shook her head. "No, that is not what I meant." She turned 275 from their spot near the extinguished coals of the fire, pointing her towards 201. "Look at her eyes, 275."

263 and 275 stood, observing 201. She sat motionless, propped up against the corner of the cage. Her eyes stared through the bars, past the makeshift camp, fixed on a point far off in the distance. Her eyes were flat, as if something within them had been lost, almost as if a part of her was missing. Her eyes appeared to take in her surroundings, yet her stare fixed on nothingness, the void reflected back in her eyes.

275 watched 201, eyes widening. "You are right, 263." She lowered her voice to a whisper. "I have not

seen anything like this before. Her eyes... she has the eyes of one who is already expired."

Reno led the Epsilon Fighters back to their transport, allowing 201 a moment outside the cage. 201 bent double, stretching her back and legs. She dropped to a crouch, taking in her surroundings. The fighting creature growled at her, a challenge in its eyes.

"You will ride with me, 201," said Reno.

"What?" called 299. "You would choose this defective? Oh, and for all my offering Officer Reno, it seems you have no taste." 299 turned to smile at her fellow Epsilon Fighters, who cheered and whistled, urging her on.

"That is enough, 299. I have not 'chosen' anyone, I wish to question the Internee, that is all. Though why I explain myself to you is beyond me." Reno led 201 to the front of the cart, pushing her up into the spot between himself and Officer Tor.

"You wound me, Officer Reno!" called 299, her voice joined by some more whistles from her fellow Epsilon Fighters. "I would like it known that my offer still stands, should your thoughts change on the matter."

"Thank you, 299. I will keep that in mind." Reno shook his head, launching himself on to the helm and clacking the reins.

201 studied his profile, watching his bald head gleam in the morning sun.

"You do not choose Internees at all, do you Officer Reno? You do not take them?"

Reno called out, urging the horses forward along the winding path by the river. The grass was flattened in places, but it would spring up before long. It was clear that this was a path rarely used, and possibly unknown to the Resident Citizens of the townships.

"At least you don't now. But once though..."

"Shut your mouth, 201."

"I am correct then," 201 said under her breath, watching Officer Tor struggle with the fighting creature, hooking the leash under his arm to keep the creature restrained.

"I said shut up."

201 was silent, watching the sun glistening off the water. The vastness of the river surprised her. She had always imagined the deserts, the mountains and rivers to be smaller than the reality of what faced her in her new surroundings, or at least her temporary surroundings until she was returned to FERTS. She could almost reach out of the cart and touch the leaves as they passed. 201 tilted her head to the sun, allowing it to warm her face.

"I have never taken an Internee," said Reno. "There was... there was one who chose me as much as I chose her."

201 blinked, eyes darting to Reno. She closed them again, seeing blue on the insides of her eyelids. When she opened her eyes, Reno looked fuzzy, surrounded by a golden light. She trained her eyes forward, giving a slight nod, waiting for the haze to clear.

"She would be over limit now, I suppose," he said.

"Where is she now?"

"I do not know where she is or what has become of her. I don't know why I am telling you this now."

201 nodded again, watching the fighting creature sniff at the earth, lurching the cart along the makeshift path.

"Alpha Field, yes?"

"How did you..."

"It doesn't matter," said 201. She watched as they passed abandoned structures, blackened and covered with leaves.

Reno's voice was soft, almost a whisper. "Yes, Alpha Field. I never saw her after that."

"You have never seen Alpha Field?"

"No I have not seen Alpha Field!" Reno shouted. "Why do you speak as if you have seen it? Only the Pinnacle Officer and birther Vassals have seen it. It is a forbidden zone for Officers."

"Of course. I understand. Why did you wish to speak to me, Reno?"

"Hmm. That is a difficult question." He huffed out a breath. "Perhaps I find you intriguing company. You seem to understand things that others do not. Perhaps I wonder how you know the things that you know."

"I dream them, most of the time," she said.

"Everybody dreams, 201," said Reno, suppressing a chuckle.

"Yes, Reno, but my dreams are real."

Reno's eyes widened.

"I hate to interrupt, Officer Reno, but could you explain to me why I am sharing the helm with an Internee? This Internee belongs in the cart with the others," said Officer Tor, adjusting his grip on the fighting creature's leash.

Officer Reno glanced past 201, catching Officer Tor's eye.

"I need to question this Internee, Officer Tor. There is much that does not make sense about the circumstances in which she was found."

"Well, if you allow me to speak plainly, Sir, it seems you have not asked the Internee any questions."

"Officer Tor, I will not have you undermining my authority on this mission." Reno raised his voice, clacking the reins. "I will not have you questioning my methods of interrogating this Internee, is that clear?"

"But Sir..."

"No! That is enough! I will hear no more on this subject!"

A jeer rose up from the cart, accompanied by whistles and shouts. "Well now, 201! It seems the Officers are fighting for your attention!" called 299.

"Maybe these new ungroomed Vassals are in demand," 263 called out, backed up by a roar from her fellow Epsilon Fighters.

"That's enough!" said Reno.

The jeers died away, leaving an uncomfortable silence. The cart rolled along the path, passing mountains and vast fields of strange plants. 201 listened to the sound of the wheels crunching over earth and grass, the labored breathing of the horses, the scrabble of the fighting creature's claws on the ground. 201 glanced at Officer Tor's feet. A small satchel lay between his ankles, the end of a scroll peeking out at her. 201 sucked in a breath. The words rose up in her mind, as clear as when she had first heard them.

*Destroy it. Destroy it all.*

"I never forgot what you told me," said 201.

Reno turned to her for a moment before locking his eyes on the path ahead.

"And what was that?"

"You told me to use this." She tapped at her forehead.

Reno's mouth twitched in a smirk.

"Those words, Reno, are the very reason I am not expired."

Reno's smile faded.

"So, do you care to tell me about it this time? And remember, 201, this is an interrogation. I trust you will leave nothing out this time."

"I was taken on horseback."

"Wait, how many mercenaries?"

*You have already said too much. Think, 201. You must not allow him to know the truth.*

"I saw five, perhaps. I could not be sure. We were separated from the group shortly after I was taken."

"And then?"

"I was taken past the suspension zone. I cannot say how far. We stopped at the first sign of the river. That is where I expired him."

Reno looked at her from the corner of his eye.

"He had a dagger on his belt. I followed my seduction manual techniques until I got hold of the dagger. Then I stabbed him, many times. He was expired before long. I was lucky to surprise him."

"Yes, you were."

"I left after he expired, hid on the ridge and watched the others take him away."

Reno pulled on the reins, slowing the horses. "The dagger you speak of. Where is it now? We found no weapons on you last night."

201 huffed out a breath, giving herself time to think. "I lost it. In the river, with the fighting creature."

"I wish to understand you, 201. Help me to understand how you are not expired after all this time."

"I was lucky. Truly fortunate, you could say."

"To survive? Out here? I find it strange that you are not expired. An Internee was not made to withstand this environment, everyone knows that."

"That is the only explanation I can give you. I believe I was truly fortunate," said 201.

"Hm, I believe you were. But there is still something I don't understand."

"What is that?" asked 201.

"I don't know yet, 201. But I will know the question when it comes to mind."

Reno clacked the reins, the horses resuming their former speed.

"Hmm. Well then, 201, it seems you did what you had to do."

"That's right," said 201, leaning back in her seat.

The image of a bloodstained silver uniform filled her vision.

"I did exactly what I had to do."

# 18

Reno shoved 201 back in the cart at their next stop. He left with Officer Tor to gather wood for a fire as light ebbed away over the mountains. 201 sat in the corner of the cart, watching through the bars as the sun dimmed behind a craggy ledge. The terrain had changed from wide open fields and forests to a rocky path, framed by mountains that contained more rock than earth.

"So, 201. Thought you'd ingratiate yourself with the Officers by flaunting your Vassal tricks?"

201 refused to look at 299. "No, 299. That is not what I was doing."

"No? Then why are the Officers fighting for your attention? I must say 201, whatever your secret is, you must share it with the rest of us, because you don't look like much to me."

201 turned to face 299. "No, 299. I did not use 'Vassal tricks', as you call them. I barely know any seduction techniques so I doubt that is what holds Reno's attention."

"Oh, now it is Reno's attention? There is no mystery there, 201. He likes you. He will choose you soon, you can be sure of that."

"You are mistaken, 299. Reno does not take Internees. He will not choose me, nor will he choose any of you."

"Why? Is there something wrong with him?" The other Epsilon Fighters began to snicker behind 299. "Something wrong with his... equipment, perhaps?" 299 laughed, head thrown back, the other Epsilon Fighters joining in with cheers and whistles.

"I would not know. But there is nothing wrong with him for not choosing a Vassal. Perhaps he is more discerning than you would like." The laughter stopped. "Perhaps he would like to wait and choose one who chooses him as well."

299 stood, towering over 201 in the cart.

"And who would that be? You?"

"No, not me," 201 said, edging away from 299.

"It seems you are most concerned with Reno's choices, 201. And now you have the Officers fighting over you when they would not bother with such matters before a Vassal came along. Is that it, 201? Are we not good enough for your Omega Circuit, with your, what was it, your 8.9 attractiveness rating?"

"No!" 201 shouted, kicking the bars in frustration. "These things, all these things we were birthed to care about, these things that keep us talking and fighting within ourselves... none of this is real! I could not care less about who Reno does or does not choose!" 201 stood to face 299, looking up at the formidable figure she had once seen wielding a scimitar in the Epsilon Games ring. "There is something wrong with this, with all of this! Can't you see that? All you do is talk of the Epsilon Games, the veneration, the choosing. Can't you see what I see? You will be expired, I will be expired and this, all of this will go on without us. These things are nothing! We are nothing to them! Nothing!"

The cart fell silent. 277 coughed, tucking her light brown hair behind her ear. 299 studied 201 as if she were a new discovery, something she had never seen before and could never comprehend.

201 pinched the bridge of her nose. When she raised her head, she found the cart of Epsilon Fighters staring at her, faces shocked, blank.

"Now I remember you. I remember that day." 277's voice seemed to come from far away. "You are the senseless one, from the ration room. Pay no more attention to this... defective. I do not understand why she has not been demoted before now. I do not wish to know."

She lowered her voice to a whisper. "Please, 299. Do not speak to her when she is like this. She... frightens me."

299 turned to 277, nodding her head and placing a hand on her shoulder.

"What was she doing out here?" said one of the Epsilon Fighters.

"Perhaps she was breaking regulation," said another.

"Yes, perhaps she was," said 299. "Do not concern yourselves, fellow Fighters. I will deal with the defective."

299 ushered the rest of the Epsilon Fighters towards the helm of the cart as she closed in on 201.

201 stood at the back of the cart, watching as 299 edged her way towards her.

The Epsilon Fighters began to stamp their feet, the sound reverberating through the wooden base of the cart and tingling through 201's body. The fighting creature outside the cage raised its head, ears twitching. It let forth a whimper, panting and baring its teeth. The feet of the Epsilon Fighters stamped, left, right, a clap of the hands and time slowed around 201.

She was in the Epsilon Games ring once more. The lights, the heat, the wood shavings gathered at her feet. Weapons glinted as they clashed before her eyes. 299 was no longer dressed in the red jumpsuit of Epsilon. She stood before 201 in her leather tunic, a shield in one hand, in the other a scimitar, her red hair wild, illuminated by the lights.

The feet stamped, left, right, a clap of the hands. The Epsilon Fighters began to shout and whistle.

201's eyes cleared in time to see 299's fist swinging towards her face.

She ducked and twisted her body, watching as 299's fist connected with the wooden bars. Cries and cheers erupted from the front of the cart, filling the silence of the once peaceful night.

*Where is Reno? What is taking them so long?*

299 turned to her, clutching her fist and flexing her fingers. "You will pay for that, whelp. I meant

what I said before. I enjoyed expiring your companion, 232."

201 took a step back, raising her hands. "I do not wish to fight you, 299."

299 grabbed at 201's jumpsuit. 201 ducked to the side, kicking out against 299's ankle and backing away.

"232 was not worthy of veneration, 201. She was as senseless as you are now. She spoke of nonsense, just as you do. And she was a coward, afraid to fight..."

"You lie!" 201 charged at 299, pushing her back against the wooden bars. "She was not afraid!" She jabbed at 299's eyes, scratched her ear and landed a blow to her midsection, which seemed to do nothing at all. 299 laughed, swinging out her arm and flinging 201 across to the other side of the cage. The bars bounced against the back of her head, dulling her senses.

299 closed in then, fists swinging at 201's face, connecting this time, glancing her eye, her cheek, the back of her head. 201 kicked out, connecting with 299's midsection again, succeeding in knocking the breath out of her, but 299 would not relent.

299 lurched towards her again, punching at the other cheek, the pain searing across the side of her face. 201 covered her face. 299 dug her fingers into 201's shoulder, ripping and tearing with her nails, pulling apart the newly-healed flesh. 201 screamed, kicking out with her feet and connecting with 299's shin. 299 closed in again, scratching and tearing. The

Epsilon Fighters stamped their feet, left, right, voices rising to a rousing cheer, their whistles echoing into the night.

"Fighters! Enough! What is the matter with you?" Reno reached inside the cart, dragging 201 away from 299's grasping hands. He locked the cage, giving the bars a smack with his fist. The Epsilon Fighters jeered, 299 leaning against the bars, taunting 201.

Reno set 201 against a log. Her eyes were unfocused, head lolling from side to side. "Officer Tor! Get some water!"

"She was right... 232 was right," 201 muttered, blood dripping from the corner of her mouth. 201's eyes locked with Reno's, her eyes blank, staring through him. "You remember what she said, don't you Reno? Don't you remember?" Reno froze, a cloth poised at 201's mouth. She could tell by the look in his eyes that is was quite possible that he did.

*One day, there will be no FERTS, no games. One day, I believe we, all of us, will be free.*

There was something there, a spark of recognition, an open, unguarded look she had not seen before in Reno, or indeed anyone she could remember in recent memory. Moments later his eyes took on their usual hard glint, making 201 wonder if she had imagined there was anything there at all.

299 glared at her through the bars of the cage, lips bloodied. Her hands curled around the bars, fingernails ringed with 201's blood.

"Remember what I said, 201. 232 was as senseless as you. I would expire her again if I could."

"Shut your mouth, 299!" shouted Reno. "There will be no more sounds from this cart tonight!"

The cart was silent, save for a low chortle that could only have come from 299.

"Come on, you have caused enough trouble for one night," said Reno, hooking his arm underneath 201 and dragging her towards the fire, setting her down on the ground and propping her against a rock. 201's head fell back, banging against the flat of the stone. The pain throbbed behind her eyes, pulse roaring in her ears.

"What did you think you were doing, 201, trying to fight 299? You must learn to know when you are outmatched."

"She did not expire me," 201 said, a laugh escaping. "Even as big as she is, she did not expire me."

"You are senseless, 201. Had I not pulled you out, she would have torn you to pieces, even without her chosen weapon. What is the matter with you?"

201 sat upright, lifting her head to catch Reno's eye. Her head throbbed from 299's punches, scattering her thoughts. She felt her defenses slipping away, the futility of her predicament closing in on her.

"I do not care any more," she whispered. "Do you understand, Officer Reno?" Her head lolled back again as she laughed, a breathy sound. "I am expired already." She smacked the rock with her palm. "I was expired before, I am expired now. Whatever I do from now on, it matters not. I am expired already."

"You make no sense, 201." His voice was stern. "Here, drink this."

201 lifted her head to drink from the flask.

"Now you need to listen to me, and properly this time. I cannot put you back in the cart tonight. Your presence is too disruptive to the other Fighters."

201 edged herself up, leaning on one elbow and propping herself on the rock to move to an upright position. She slumped forward, hair hanging down over her face. Her speech was slurred but she repeated her attempts, pushing to get the words out. "I... I am not a Fighter, remember? Merely... I was a merely a trainee. Not up for Fighter selection. I did not wish to be a Vassal and yet I was promoted. And now I have a scar so I must fight once more. I am none of these things, Reno. That is what they do not understand."

Reno handed her a cloth, placing it in her palm. "The way you speak now, this is why you were not promoted to Fighter, 201."

201 struggled to raise her head, her fist clenching around the fabric.

"No, Reno." She wiped at her mouth, tucking the cloth in her pocket. "No, that is not why. Tell me why."

"I cannot answer that." Reno handed her some more water.

201 coughed, spitting out the water and a little blood. "Perhaps I already know, Reno. Tell me."

Reno seated himself next to 201 on the rock, watching the flames of the fire burn brighter as

Officer Tor struggled to load up more logs and kindling.

His voice was low when he spoke, too low for Officer Tor to hear. "Because it would have been a waste."

201 tilted her head, attempting to focus her eyes on the ground. Her vision was blurred, more on the right side than the left. Her head throbbed, an ache running through her neck and shoulders.

201's voice was rough as she cleared her throat to speak. "What do you mean, a waste?"

"The Epsilon Fighters, they are trained to fight," said Reno. "It is all they know. But you are not made for this. I do not know what you are made for."

201 lifted her head, attempting to keep it steady. "I can fight, you know."

"Yes, I know you can fight. You expired a mercenary, after all. But it is not all you can do. I have not seen this before. Not for some time, anyway."

"And you wish to... observe? To study me? If I am returned to FERTS, they will study me, scan me, tear me apart and they will send me to Zeta. There is no difference, it makes no difference to me now. You talk of waste, but this is what will happen."

Reno stood, looming over her. "How dare you say this... what do you mean *if* you are returned to FERTS?"

201 looked up at Reno through matted hair. Her voice was low and steady, despite her raspy throat. "I mean that I have come to the end. Whatever happens now, I will not return. You may wish to expire me

now, just to be sure, but I will not return to FERTS. This is a choice I have made for myself."

Reno straightened, posture rigid. "It is admirable to believe that you will be venerated in your service to FERTS, expired in battle against the mercenaries. A fitting end, yes?"

201 shook her head. "That is not what I meant. It is not the method, it is the choice that I have made. My choice."

"Vassals do not choose. You know that."

"I am not a Vassal. I am not a Fighter. I am none of these things. Perhaps there is no longer a name for what I am."

Reno picked up a small branch, tossing it on to the flames. "You trouble me, 201. You make me think. You make me wonder about things."

"Perhaps it is because I am like you, Reno. I am just like you. There is nothing for you to study."

Reno smirked at her. "I am an Officer, 201. You are an Internee. You forget yourself."

"No, Reno. I forget nothing. You see this?" She held out her hand, muddied and red around the knuckles. "This is my blood. It is the same as your blood."

"We are not the same, 201."

"We are exactly the same! We eat, we sleep, we bleed and we *feel*, just as you do. And some of us, we dream. Those Fighters, they will play, and fight, and speak as you wish them to speak, the Vassals will simper and pander and behave as Vassals are expected to behave, but inside, in here..." She tapped her forehead. "We are all the same. This, this is what has been lost."

Reno stared at her, mouth open but saying nothing.

"I was birthed in FERTS, and perhaps now you will be required to make sure I am expired, but I will not expire within those walls. So what I say now means nothing. I will be sent to Zeta now, I know it. You have no choice and 299, 263 and the others... they will report this if you do not."

"Keep your voice down!" Reno hissed. He knelt before 201, lowering his voice. "Help me to understand, 201. Why must you do everything the way you do? The way you behave... it makes no sense. You do not follow orders, you do not observe regulation."

"I cannot lie about this to you, Reno. I do not know why this is, but what I have seen, it changes things. I cannot go back, not after being fr... not after being out here, not after what I have seen. But you have your orders, nothing can change that now."

"This makes no sense. You see things. You knew about... you know things that cannot possibly be known. Things that some of the Officers do not know. Things that I myself do not know. How?"

201 was quiet, eyes half-closed, watching the fire.

"How do you see what you see? Were you always this way?" Reno gripped her arm.

"Let go of me."

Reno released his grip, watching as 201 winced, clenching her fist.

"Tell me, 201," Reno said, his voice firm. "I must know. I will not ask again."

"All I will say is that something happened. Something I do not wish to speak of. I will never speak of it, not to you, not to anyone."

"You must tell me. I demand it," said Reno. "I will wait, if necessary, until you tell me what I need to know. Perhaps the fighting creature can help you find your voice."

The creature's ears twitched at Reno's words. It snarled, locking eyes with 201.

"You want to know? This is what you want?" 201 said, wiping a trickle of blood from her mouth with a sneer. "Fine. I will give you what you want." 201 took a shaky breath. "I was 12Y when Officer Jorg..."

*"Shh. Don't you dare make a sound. Someone will hear and then you will be punished."*

The maddening tickle of his thinning blonde hair against her throat.

*"And you know what the punishment will be, don't you, little one?"*

201 squeezed her eyes shut, fighting back the feeling of choking, looking anywhere but up at the Officer above her, wanting to run, to escape...

"No." She clenched her fist. "That is all I will say of this. I cannot speak of it. When it happened... that was the first time I was aware of it, of what I could do. That was the moment when my mind first split from my body."

Reno leaned forward to watch the flames, avoiding 201's eyes.

"I wanted to get away, Reno." 201 blew out a breath, listening to the sounds of water running in the distance. "I wanted to get away so much but I couldn't..."

201 watched Reno's hands shake as they rested on his knees. He clenched his fists, his spine rigid.

"I found a way out," she whispered. "I could escape, in my mind, at least." She attempted a grin. "My mind escaped, even when my body could not. I was 12Y, Reno."

She looked over to see Reno's eyes wide, shining, staring at the fire. He tried to speak, then closed his mouth, shaking his head.

"Ah. You did not know. Of course, how could you know? Most of the Officers know little of what is happening, they know less about the true nature of the facility. One hand feeds the other, but one does not know where the other goes. Zeta Officers are separated from Omega, from Beta, Epsilon and Kappa. The Pinnacle Officer speaks of things that are believed to be true, but you will find, just as I did, that it is not the case. Now the Pinnacle Officer is expired, and so soon another one rises in his place."

"Do not speak of the Pinnacle Officer in this way. You speak too much, you have already said too much."

"So I have been told. And so I will be told again. But it does not end there. Nor does it end for the other Internees. It will never end."

"I warn you, 201. You cannot speak like this."

"It's over, Reno. I do not care anymore."

"If you speak of this, you know what will happen."

"What will happen? What could be worse than what I have already..." 201 laughed. "I suppose they will send me to Zeta? Do you know, Reno, are you aware of the processes, the procedures? Are you aware of what really happens in Zeta Circuit?"

"Do not speak of this, 201. I am warning you for the last time. Shut your mouth."

"No," 201 swayed in towards Reno, studying his face. "No, you do not know. They have not told you either."

"Enough! I will hear no more of this!" He pushed 201 to her feet, leading her down towards the cart. 201's head swam, her blood rushing through her body and making her nauseous.

She shrugged him off, turning to face him, swaying on her feet.

"They burn them, Reno." 201's eyes met his. "Even the little ones."

"Officer Tor! Rope!" shouted Reno, avoiding 201's eyes.

"Think of that when you sleep tonight, Reno. I see it in my dreams, night after night. Each time the faces are different but the result is always the same."

"Not another word, 201."

Officer Tor rummaged in the front of the cart, alighting to land next to Reno.

"Officer Tor, secure 201 to the base of the cart. If she tries to move during the night, you have my permission to release the fighting creature." Reno left without another word.

Officer Tor wound the rope around 201, securing her to the undercarriage of the cart. 201 slumped back, eyes closing, her strength leaving her. He tried to ignore the sounds at first, as 201 whispered nonsensical words under her breath. She spoke of bones and fires and a pit, of logs of wood, the metal of an axe in a sea of orange. Officer Tor leaned his head closer to 201, her whispers now barely audible.

"They think they will be venerated when they fall," she whispered, head lolling to the side. "Bones in a pit, that's all they are."

Officer Tor shook his head. "Quiet," he said. "It is because of you that I do not get to sleep tonight."

201 leaned up, gripping the front of his uniform. She moved her head to whisper in his ear. "The bones. They are hollow, just like us." 201 sighed, falling back to rest her head in the wooden ledge at the side of the cart.

Officer Tor backed off, prising her fingers from the fabric, a scowl crossing his face.

201 exhaled, her words spoken softly under her breath. "They are still there. All of them. Still there. They don't know..."

# 19

The cart passed unusual rock formations, rings and patterns marking the sides of the towering stone walls. Some of the patterns looked familiar to 201, but she was certain she had not seen anything like them before. One of the markings appeared to have been carved by hand. There was no way that such a symbol could be naturally occurring in such a remote and secluded place as this.

299 kicked 201's shin, barking out at laugh when 201 clutched her leg. 201 took a deep breath, looking out between the bars, ignoring 299's attempts to get her attention.

201 looked more closely at the symbol scratched in the stone. It appeared to have been carved with a tool, perhaps another rock, although 201 could not be certain. The symbol was unlike anything she had seen before, either in dreams or her waking state.

The symbol started as a curved line, gradually winding outwards from the middle until it just... stopped. 201's eyes widened as they passed the rock, following the path of the symbol with her eyes.

*This. This. It is important. This means something.*

"What's the matter, 201? Thinking about Reno, hmm? Or perhaps Officer Tor? I must say I would enjoy either... or both." The cart broke out in laughter at 299's words.

201 ignored them, following the symbol again and again with her eyes. It seemed to her that it was a path, leading from the middle to outside. It felt... familiar. It was as if it told a story of some kind. 201 thought of the nights spent alone in her chambers at FERTS with nothing but her own mind to keep her company. To 201, this was a symbol of hope. Perhaps it had different meanings for whoever saw it. Perhaps the meaning was lost to all who had seen it, a long time ago.

"From the inside." She traced the symbol in the air with her finger, muttering to herself. "From the inside to the outside. Could that be what it means? A path?"

"What are you talking about, 201? You are making no sense, as usual," 263 snapped at her. The Epsilon Fighters began talking amongst themselves, speaking of veneration and the adulation they would receive for defeating the mercenaries who dared to strike against FERTS. The words were always the same, always the same, whether it was Epsilon, Beta or Omega Circuit, the words were repeated, almost as if the Pinnacle Officer himself were speaking them. 201 wondered why she had not noticed this before. The words, no matter what they were or who spoke them came from one place and once place only. FERTS.

201 tuned out the voices, focusing on the symbol in her mind. She wished to carve it deep into the wood of the cart, but there was nothing she could have used without drawing attention to herself. She contented

herself with tracing the symbol in her mind, watching as it appeared behind her eyes. She drew the symbol again and again, making sure she would remember it so she could keep it within herself, locked away. It felt strong, protective somehow.

That night, 201 slept in the cart with the Epsilon Fighters. 299 had made a declaration not to attack 201 in her sleep, and 201 had been forced to do the same.

The thought of doing such a thing had occurred to her many times, though the other Epsilon Fighters would never allow her to leave the cart after she had expired one of their own. Of course, Reno would not take kindly to a trainee expiring one of his most celebrated Fighters. He would be forced to expire her in order to appease the Epsilon Fighters. It was clear that 299 was not worth it and no matter how briefly satisfying the thought may have been, she wasn't sure that she could have gone through with it. It mattered not that she had done it once before. It did not necessarily mean she would wish to do it again, especially not while there were other, more important matters to consider.

A plan was forming around the edges of her consciousness, not yet solid, unformed. She allowed her mind to make connections and compare options. It was not her business to interfere with the process. It was time to watch, and listen.

Later that night 201 felt herself slipping off to sleep. The Epsilon Fighters were motionless, 299's snores reverberating from the other end of the cart.

All 201 could see at first was the strange symbol from the rock.

She started from the middle, the same as before, following the line as it angled ever so slightly outwards, around and around until 201 felt almost dizzy with the sensation. The symbol spoke to her. It did not use words, as one might speak to a companion. It was more of a feeling, a sense, something from the past, so long ago, yet it seemed as if it was real, it was now, and somehow she felt this symbol was for her to see and understand, as if it were meant for her alone.

The symbol disappeared, scattering like leaves in a strong breeze. She found herself in a midst of a group, gathered around a fire. There were so many here, more than 201 had ever seen outside of FERTS. She was sure that the faces she saw were no longer here, expired perhaps, she could not be certain, but felt it to be true.

The first thing she noticed was that there were no insignia, nothing to indicate Y numbers or anything like that. It was also clear that they, at least many of them, were over limit. This was something she had not seen with her own eyes, not in the real, the tangible reality as she understood it. She had seen a 25Y once, but that was only for a brief moment. Outside her dreams and the travels in her mind, she had not seen a group so large, defying any known category she could find for them.

The faces smiled and repeated strange words, joining hands and gathering strange plants, placing them one by one on the fire as they spoke of things that had no meaning to 201. They were words 201 had not heard before. 201 wondered if others used those words, if they were in use today or if they were lost forever.

One of them drew the symbol on the ground, the shape appearing in the dirt as she dragged the stick behind her, walking outwards from the middle of the symbol.

Once the symbol was drawn, the others...

*Women*

Yes, that is what they were. Women, perhaps the ones that Officer Titan had once spoken about, the ones from long ago that may have been like her in some way. 201 knew they were no longer here. This was just a remnant of what had once been, before the Pinnacle Officer, before FERTS.

They seemed so different to anything 201 had seen before, so unlike her, but perhaps that was just perception, conditioning, what she had been taught since being birthed in FERTS. She was not taught to understand such things and yet she longed to be a part of this... whatever this was.

The group joined hands. They raised their voices together, repeating the words in unison. They walked to various positions around the symbol, seating themselves on the ground and simply closing their eyes. 201 watched, waiting for something, a sign that something was happening, but it never came.

The group just sat together, eyes closed.

201 was confused, focusing on their faces, but none of them moved. They remained still, as if they were waiting for something.

201 projected her awareness to join the group, sitting in an empty spot near the symbol. She kept her eyes open. None of the group acknowledged her presence.

She tried squinting her eyes, closing them and opening them again.

Nothing.

She tried keeping her eyes open, softening her gaze to allow for peripheral movement. That was the moment everything changed. She no longer saw a group of... women sitting around a symbol. Instead she saw a glow emanating from the symbol, streams of light, green, red, pink and orange stretching out from each of the women and intertwining with each other. The streams, no... the essences from the women joined together, winding up into the night sky where thousands of stars peered down at them. Their combined essence grew stronger, more unified and 201 began to understand. Now, right now, they were seeing, just as she did. The stronger the connection, the stronger the messages, the stronger the images that filtered through the group, streaming to each of the women seated on the ground.

*I am one of them.*

Perhaps there were others like her. Perhaps she would find another in the camp who would understand, perhaps even in FERTS, that is, if they had not already been sent to Zeta for being a defective.

Maybe she was not the only one.

A voice rose up in her head, as if in answer to a question she had not yet asked. A voice she did not recognize, but knew all the same.

*Before I was expired I did not see. Now I see everything. I am bound to him 201, just as he is now bound to you.*

She found herself staring through glass, a rust-tinged liquid filtering her view. She was in Wilcox's chambers. A wardrobe, a keyhole, a sliver of light meant only for blue eyes.

*My eyes are blue and I see everything.*

She watched through the murky liquid within the jar, Pinnacle Officer Wilcox's sweaty form filling her consciousness, making her nauseous. He writhed on the bed, his bald head glistening, peeking from the coverings. A Beta Internee lay beneath him, eyes clenched shut.

The voice returned, filling 201's senses.

*Thinks he is so clever, making me watch like this. To him, it is parts, pieces, sections that make up the whole. He believes the eyes still see. But he would be wrong. I am Beth, and I see everything. I am the breeze that blows through the forest near the suspension zone, I am the rocks, the pebbles, the shrubs, the craggy mountains and winding streams. I am the forest, the creatures, the sky, the sliver of the moon at night, the orb when it is full. I am the stars,*

*the blanket, the canopy of life from which we began.*
*I am Beth, and I see everything.*

201 gasped, spinning her awareness to face the sound. She saw a glass jar, a jar filled with liquid that burned the senses. The blue eyes floating within, bobbing, lid tightly secured, clear, precise label faded with time.

Beth #1. 26Y.

# 20

Pinnacle Officer Cerberus surveyed his new office. He had removed all traces of Pinnacle Officer Wilcox save for one. The jar he had found within the wardrobe had amused him. So, Pinnacle Officer Wilcox had a weakness after all. It was pathetic, really. How Wilcox could be so affected, so sentimental about a common Vassal, if indeed that was what she was. He placed the odd memento on a shelf, a heartening reminder of how an Officer, even the Pinnacle Officer, could be compromised by attachment. He pondered the jar, suspecting that Wilcox had enjoyed her eyes on him throughout the day, and he supposed, during the nights as well. What a curious desire, he thought. The former Pinnacle Officer had been... unusual in his thinking, to say the least. Whatever his reasons may have been, they were now lost, along with much of his original vision. Yet Cerberus made it his duty to carry on the legacy of Wilcox, no matter how strange, as Wilcox had brought peace to the Forkstream Territories. The system had worked up until now, and he would strive to continue the development of Wilcox's vision while adding some improvements of his own.

Pinnacle Officer Cerberus returned to his desk, formulating the plans for the new Ward Beacon. The old model had been clumsy, ineffective. Efficiency was required now. Pinnacle Officer Wilcox had often been set in his thinking. Once something worked, it was not to be tampered with, and this had been an effective system, until now.

The plans for the implant markers were fascinating. A giddy feeling welled up within him as he turned each page, revealing the inner processes, the information that he had coveted for so long, but had never had the privilege to observe.

To his annoyance, he learned that the implant markers were old technology, surplus from a stockpile amassed during the war. There would be no more manufacturing of such items, not at this time. There would have to be an alternative method to solve the security problems of the facility.

He wondered if it was possible to approach the challenge from the opposite perspective. The implant markers were a receiver. That was how Pinnacle Officer Wilcox had engineered the system. The improvements would need to be applied to the Ward Beacon itself. One improvement to the Ward Beacon could provide a multitude of benefits for the facility.

Cerberus ran a hand through his hair. He had much to learn from the Pinnacle Officer, despite his own abilities. Pinnacle Officer Wilcox was a scientist and a surgeon who possessed a brilliant mind, there was no doubt of that, but he was no engineer. Cerberus knew engineering. It had been his chosen field before the war, and coupled with his brief experience in the military, it was clear that his approach would be different to that of the former Pinnacle Officer.

Pinnacle Officer Wilcox had been adamant about the removal of all traces of the instruments of war, the establishment of peace and the removal of the necessity for powerful weapons, but this was the point on which Cerberus differed. Where there were times of peace, there would be times of war, that was his understanding. Despite Pinnacle Officer Wilcox's optimism, Cerberus knew that peace would not last forever in the Forkstream Territories. Perhaps he could bring another perspective to the issues with the Ward Beacon.

The Ward Beacon could be modified perhaps, as Officer Cerberus understood the principles involved. Perhaps a modification to reduce power usage and to activate for longer periods. Could the Ward Beacon be used in another way? Perhaps to exert more control over the Internees. Now that would be an achievement, he mused.

The beauty pill was another concern. Control the temperament of the Internees and the need for security was lessened, just as Pinnacle Officer Wilcox had engineered the system. There was no need for weapons, for restraints. The pill contained a blend of hormones, the balance carefully controlled to keep the population docile and their emotions dulled. If only there was a way, somewhere in the myriad of notes before him, that he could find the hormone that further increased docility, malleability, something to guarantee the dutiful compliance of the Internee population.

And on the other hand, and this, this was something he was sure the Pinnacle Officer had not considered. Could there be some way to increase the impulses of the fighting instinct inherent in the Internees in Epsilon? If so, why had this not been achieved? What the Pinnacle Officer did not understand, brilliant though he had been, was the clarity of the facts that now lay before him.

Officer Cerberus sat back in his chair, exhilarated by the thought forming in his mind. Why attempt to recruit an army when the very resources lay already under your control?

There would be a frequency, he knew this to be true. Pinnacle Officer Wilcox's notes lay before him, painstakingly recorded, every frequency tested on Internee implant markers. The emotional response, the physiological effects, all charted in great detail. This knowledge, this gift, Cerberus corrected, would be the key to the continuation of FERTS, he just needed to pinpoint, to isolate the correct frequency for the desired effect.

Officer Cerberus exhaled, running his fingers through his hair. He believed he had found it, and now was the time to test out his theory. This was his chance. He would not continue the work of Pinnacle Officer Wilcox. This would be an insult to the Pinnacle Officer, his veneration, and his legacy. Instead, he would reshape it, actualize the vision of the great

Pinnacle Officer himself. He would not merely maintain the order that Pinnacle Officer Wilcox had created. This time, it was his chance to bring forth the vision, seemingly out of reach, but so close he could almost touch it. He would refine the processes, reshape the order, and ultimately, improve on it.

# 21

The days passed slowly for 201, the blackened, vine-covered ruins of former dwellings dotting the landscape. She had asked Reno if she could ride in the front of the cart again but he had refused, a shake of his head the only response. He had not spoken to her since the fight with 299. The night when she had said too much.

*How could I have let myself speak like that? What is the matter with me?*

The day had begun with the FERTS requital, the Epsilon Internees answering dutifully in unison. 201 had kept her mouth shut, ignoring the Epsilon Fighters and remaining silent during the requital. She rested against the wooden bars, gripping them with both hands.

*We're getting close. Too close.*

201 looked up, watching the landscape change as the cart continued on its path. A feeling welled up within her, the feeling she had experienced when she had found the symbol, the feeling she remembered when she saw the camp in her mind for the first time. It was no longer a feeling of excitement alone. This time it was mixed with uncertainty, a clench in the base of her stomach. This time she was not in her

quarters at FERTS, this time what she saw was real, unfolding before her eyes, and she could do nothing but watch as the cart took them closer, ever closer.

*It was never meant to be like this. We are too close. It's too late. The fighting creature has brought us to them.*

Reno had been quiet, his silence grating on Officer Tor's nerves.

"It's taking longer than we expected, Sir. Do you think we are on the right path?" asked Officer Tor. His forehead creased as he watched the fighting creature scurry from side to side, yanking at the lead.

Reno did not answer. He flicked the reins, guiding the horses through the overgrown terrain. The cart wound through seemingly endless fields, past wild plants and flowers blooming and stretching out from the banks of the Elan river. The fighting creature had tired on occasion, becoming disoriented with the enticing new sights and scents. They had rested until the creature had regained its strength, taking off towards a wooded grove with renewed vigor. The cart bumped its way through a long clearing, flanked on either side by the shade of staggered rows of trees. Reno watched as the creature sniffed along the path, the leash flapping against its flank. The trees filed past in the corner of his eye, glimpses of the Elan river peeking through the thick, enveloping branches. Before long, the trees opened out into sharp ridges of rock, the cart teetering along rocky ledges, winding down towards the plains at the base of the cliff.

The warmth dropped away as they reached the plains and before long they were passing through towering caves, weaving through the shadows of ridged walls that arched above their heads. Piles of timber lay scattered along the overgrown path, a jumbled mess of charred beams, frames of dwellings and something that may have once resembled a hall. These were the markers of a former township, thought Reno, once thriving and full of activity. Remains of rusted vehicles lay beside the path. Grasses grew inside their husks, snaking around the wheels, the blackness of the rubber standing out starkly against the relentless invasion of nature.

The fighting creature veered from the path, the lead stretching out from the cart, jolting Officer Tor to his left.

"Whoa!" Reno drew back on the reins, pulling the horses to an abrupt halt. Officer Tor grabbed his double pointed spear, following the creature's movements as it charged towards a waterfall. The sounds of rushing water hissed above them, a mist cooling the air. The creature circled, darting from one rock to the next, scampering along mosses, growling and barking at the droplets as they fell to the pool below.

"What do you think?" asked Officer Tor, watching the creature's disordered sprinting, revealing no discernible path in its movements.

"The scent remains here. The creature will find its way out."

The creature sat on a rock, howling and whining, huddling itself to the cold stone. After a time, its whines ceased and it settled on the flat surface, resting its paws under its jaw.

"I'm not so sure about that," said Officer Tor, securing the creature's lead to a nearby tree and returning the spear to the cart.

Reno followed the trail they had taken, the unbroken line of passage before the creature had diverted from the path. He made his way over to the ridge, dropping to a crouch when he caught sight of it. He crawled to the edge, peering over the top.

The twin cliffs framed a path leading through to a broad valley, modest dwellings dotting the paths expanding from a central point. Smoke rose from chimneys over the vast fields laden with crops, the cleared plains surrounded by cliffs and waterfalls. He took note of the largest dwelling nestled by the waterfall, the wooden structure surrounded by wild flowers.

A gasp sounded from Officer Tor behind him.

"Get down!" Reno whispered, pulling Officer Tor to the ground beside him. Officer Tor's eyes were wide, mouth open on a slow exhale.

"This is it. We've found their camp. The adulation of FERTS will be ours," Officer Tor whispered beside him.

Reno ran a hand over his lip, now damp with sweat. He noticed the set of fields at the back, strange, yet familiar in some way. Reno shook his head. His eyes tracked the layout, pinpointing the location of structures, the open areas, the placement of the fields. This did not have the layout of a small village, nor did it look like any township Reno had ever seen.

"This is no camp, Officer Tor," Reno muttered, watching the smoke curl to the sky.

He scanned the bare fields, lines of identical sacks dotting the far edges. The lines of sacks were precise, straight lines facing a small cabin too small for habitation but just the right size for storage. Looking at the field, the sacks and the storage cabin, he no longer needed to imagine what might be kept in there.

Reno was the High Training Room Officer at Epsilon. He was the administrator of weapons and skills preparation for the Epsilon Games. And Reno was no fool. He knew a training ground when he saw it.

# 22

The fire wavered, sending the smoke away from the cliff's edge at the rear of the camp.

201 noted that Reno was wise enough to make sure they were downwind from the camp before even considering starting a fire. 201 was not surprised, in fact she had expected nothing less. Reno had not been appointed High Training Room Officer for no reason. She considered that at times they thought alike, their minds moving along the same path, though with different goals in mind. The difference was that Reno was more predictable, at least that was her impression so far. But she was careful not to underestimate the mind of a highly ranked Officer. That would be a mistake, and could be a costly one if she was not careful.

This night was darker than most. Only a sliver of moon was visible, making it more difficult to gather wood. A crunching thud emerged from the grove of trees as Officer Tor tripped for the third time, bending to pick up the sticks he had dropped. A curse rang out through the trees.

"Officer Tor? What is taking so long?" Reno called, prodding the fire with a large stick. The fire was new, producing a fair amount of smoke, but not yet established enough to provide much heat. The nights had grown colder over the last few days and Reno was not accustomed to sleeping on hard ground. The fire was a necessity, but he was prepared to go without if the wind began to blow in the opposite direction. The need for stealth was paramount at this time.

"I can't see too well out here, Sir. I won't be a moment, just gathering some more wood for the fire."

263 prodded 201 from her position at the back of the cage, jolting her from her thoughts. "So, 201, are you excited about tomorrow?"

201 held back the stream of feelings flooding her consciousness. She could barely contain the rush of sensations that passed too quickly for her to experience them one by one. She thought for a moment for the right words but no words came to her.

"I cannot wait to earn the adulation of FERTS," said 263, her eyes shining with excitement. "The Pinnacle Officer will be so proud of us. And those of us who do not... those who are expired, well, they will be venerated, as is fitting for an Epsilon Fighter, wouldn't you agree?"

201 said nothing, watching as Officer Tor brought more wood from the tree line to hand over to Reno. Reno piled the wood on the fire, watching the flames brighten. She scratched her outstretched leg. The cart was cramped and she had not had much of a chance to stretch her legs, except to use the cover of the forest with 299 standing guard, for want of a bathroom.

She looked up to see 263 watching her, awaiting her reply. She scanned back through the conversation, trying to remember what it was 263 had been saying before she had lost her concentration. She took another quick look at the fire, the position of the Officers and the location of the fighting creature.

"Yes, 263, of course. I agree." She gathered her thoughts, turning and smiling her presentation smile. "I cannot wait for tomorrow." 263 smiled back, her smile faltering when she saw the look in 201's eyes.

Later that night, after Officers Tor and Reno had fallen asleep, 201 glanced around the cage, watching for any signs of movement. 299 snored in her usual fashion, mouth open, her breath fogging in the night air.

She turned to 263, who had curled in on herself due to the cold, her breaths steady and even. 275's chest rose and fell, almost in time with 263's. 201 scanned her eyes over the rest of the Epsilon Fighters, confirming that they were all asleep, huddled together inside the cart.

She peered through the bars at the fighting creature. Its face was smoothed out, huffs of contentment escaping every now and then, its wide mouth curved up in something resembling a smile. 201 shuddered. She almost preferred the creature with its usual snarl. The hint of a smile made it look almost harmless, as if she could reach out and stroke its fur, but she knew that was impossible. A single touch to the creature would set it off barking, and she would most likely lose a finger or two. She contented herself with the illusion of peace, watching the creature lie dormant, showing the part of itself that would never be seen once the morning light hit its features.

201 edged herself to the front corner of the cart, perching on the bench seat. She sat with her leg outstretched, resting her elbow against the wooden bars. Every night it was the same, the plan formulating through her mind, taking shape without pushing it in one way or another. 201 was aware of the part of her mind that did not take instruction, the part of her mind that observed, noted, and planned. The difference was that the final night had come to her far sooner than expected. There were no more nights to plan. This was it, whether she was ready or not.

*What do you think you are doing, 201?*

Get out of my head Wilcox, she thought. She had the urge to speak, but sound, any sound that was not absolutely necessary was out of the question. Not tonight. Not this time. Tonight she would be silent.

*Thought you could escape from us, 201? I am bound to you, like B... like she said. You cannot escape from FERTS. You are an Internee and you will always be an Internee. FERTS lives within you. As long as I have a voice, FERTS will live within you, never forget that.*

201 ignored the voice, reaching down, unfastening the clasps on her jumpsuit. She ran her hand down her leg, stopping when she found it.

The cloth was tied around her thigh, securing a sturdy stick with a forked end, hidden beneath the fabric of her jumpsuit. She untied the stick and pulled it out by inches, left hand, right hand, left again, until it sat across her knees. She glanced around. The fighting creature made a grunting sound, shifting its head to rest on its paws. 299 snored louder, the droning sound rattling in her ears. She took a final look around at the sleeping faces before making her move.

She edged the stick out of the bars, reaching for the fire. The stick fell short of its destination. 201 pressed up against the bars, her arm outstretched all the way to the shoulder. The bars pinched her skin but she pushed further until the stick found its mark. A glowing ember dislodged from the darkened coals, rolling towards the cart. 201 stopped it with the fork of the stick before it skittered out of range.

She dragged the ember, edging it towards herself as it rolled left, then right before tumbling into her outstretched hand. She caught it in the middle of the cloth before it could change direction. Gathering the ember in the cloth, she pushed her body against the bars, whirling the cloth in a backwards arc, gathering momentum with each pass. The bars knocked against her arm, but she continued to swing, ignoring the ache spreading through her shoulder.

She kept the cloth swinging, watching the fibers glow from within, the ember beginning to crackle and glimmer in the middle of the bundle. Another pass and the cloth would catch fire. This was it. She would not get another chance this time.

She released her grip, letting the cloth fly open at the lowest point of her swing, watching the ember sail across the stretch of ground between the cart and the cliff. She dropped the bundle, patting it against the ground, smothering the sparks that remained glowing within the cloth.

She could hear Pinnacle Officer Wilcox's voice screaming in her head. His words merged into one, garbling and twisting as she tuned them out. She sat back against the bars, squeezing the warm cloth in her hands. The scent of burning cloth reached her nostrils. She watched the faces of the sleeping Epsilon Fighters, noting that they had not moved, at least not yet. She watched the edge of the cliff for any signs that her plan had worked, sensing nothing.

*What did you expect?*

Now all that was left to do was wait. 201 breathed out, watching her breath leave in clouds through the bars. Her nose was cold, the tips of her fingers beginning to numb. She rubbed her hands together, placing them over her face.

There were no sounds from below. How had she thought this could work? There would be no more chances after tonight. It had to work. She strained to see past the edge of the cliff. Nothing. Not that she could see anything of importance from her vantage point.

She shuffled to the edge of the bars once more, reaching out with the stick for another attempt. She had almost reached another glowing ember, shifting the blackened coals out of the way when she heard it.

The sound was faint, almost too soft for her to hear. If she had not been listening, ears trained for the most insignificant of sounds, she might not have heard it.

It was a slight crackle, similar to the distant sound of feet walking over branches, but 201 knew that this was not what she had heard. This was a fire. A little fire perhaps, but a fire.

201 exhaled in a rush, tucking the stick underneath the cart and leaning back against the bars. She refastened her jumpsuit, thankful for the meagre warmth provided by the barrier against the cold.

The fighting creature snorted, a thin stream of drool escaping from the corner of its mouth. 299 snored, her mouth hanging open. Officers Tor and Reno lay motionless on the other side of the fire. She squinted her eyes and detected the slight rise and fall of Reno's chest as he slept.

201 watched the moon. It looked different tonight, the slim crescent streaked with clouds.

She tried to focus her energies on the camp, trying to lock in on their collective essence. She had to know if her plan had been effective.

Nothing. She tried again, a dark energy, solid, like a wall, rose up, blocking her attempts.

*Wilcox.*

She tried once more, attempting to push the barrier from her mind. It was no use. The presence of Wilcox was an unwelcome development. It mattered not. What was done was done. If Wilcox was angry, then she supposed it could be a good sign. She tried to imagine the camp, the faces she would see, the brightness of spirit that she had hoped to emulate one day.

An image formed in her mind. It was a group settled around a fire, animated with laughter. They drank a strange concoction, filling their mugs and chattering, their voices blending into one. 201 observed the easy way they interacted with one another, the unspoken gestures, the comfortable way they talked and laughed. Their mannerisms suggested a sense of unity and trust that she had not experienced before.

*See?*

Wilcox's voice was harsh with disdain.

*You could never have what they have. You can never be like these rogue defectives. You may think you are different, 201, but you are still an Internee. I should have liked to study you. If only I had known what went on in that little head of yours.*

You would have taken me apart, she thought. You would have taken me apart piece by piece, just as you did to Beth.

*Well, yes. I suppose you are right. Of course, we cannot have the likes of you polluting the Internee pool, defective.*

You forget yourself, Wilcox, she thought, careful not to speak her words out loud. You are no longer in control.

*That is where you are wrong, 201. A man such as myself does not lose control. It is merely transferred.*

You mean that when I expired you, another rose in your place. 201 huffed, rubbing her hands together, warming them with her breath.

*Now you are beginning to understand. You thought you fought against one. But you cannot fight an idea. You cannot fight my design. It is too powerful. FERTS now lives and breathes under my watchful eye. You have achieved nothing, 201.*

I expired you, she thought.

*It matters not. FERTS lives on. You know, for one who thinks they are so smart, you are really quite dense, hardly approaching my level of understanding. But that is to be expected. A Vassal is not prized for having thoughts. Look at yourself, 201. Your face... bruised and swollen like the faces of the Fighters at the Epsilon Games. You have not bathed in days. Your hair is matted and your skin is dry from the sun. You were not made for this. This wild environment is no place for a Vassal. You require direction. You require the provision and protection of FERTS in order for you to reach your potential as a Vassal.*

I am not a Vassal, she thought. No matter how you might appraise me, it matters not. You underestimate my determination to finish this.

*You cannot escape FERTS. It lives within you, as I do. You will find this to be true soon enough, Internee.*

She curled in on herself, blocking out the sound of Wilcox's voice.

Another sound rang out. It sounded like a night bird, though 201 had never heard this particular call. These sounds were still unusual to her ears.

She willed her mind to relax, attempting to rest for the few short hours until first light. She focused her attention on trying to calm her breathing and to quiet the throb of her heart as it beat faster and faster.

# 23

Pinnacle Officer Cerberus stood before an Epsilon Internee with his papers spread out before him, secured with heavy quartz. The testing room was cold, sterile. The Internee sat, strapped to a chair, her eyes wide, the hair at her temples plastered with sweat. The Epsilon Internee was a trainee Fighter, one month's training in total. She was dressed only in an undershirt and undergarments, her skin pebbled from the cold.

"Hold still," said Pinnacle Officer Cerberus. The Internee struggled, shaking her head from side to side. A fighting creature lay at the end of a chain, curled in the corner of the room with a thin trail of drool escaping from its fangs.

He referred to his notes. If his calculations were correct, he had isolated the correct frequency for his purposes. He could feel a sense of his impending success. This would be a triumph for FERTS, a continuation of the former Pinnacle Officer's great work in keeping peace while maintaining a level of protection. The Officers had no need to arm themselves, this would only lead to what Pinnacle Officer Wilcox termed 'The baser instincts', preventing the Officers from becoming actualized. No, with this new system, the protection of FERTS would come from the Epsilon Internees themselves. Bred for fighting, it made perfect sense, the idea encapsulating the kind of beauty and simplicity that he had come to associate with FERTS. Pinnacle Officer Wilcox would be proud, he thought. At least, he believed it to be true. He shuffled his notes, readying himself for the ultimate test of the frequency's effect on the Epsilon Internee's implant marker.

"I said hold still," Pinnacle Officer Cerberus repeated, placing a small dagger in the hands of the Internee. Her eyes were questioning, her delicate arms shaking as they gripped the dagger, unsure of what to do next.

"Now, you may feel a little sting."

Pinnacle Officer Cerberus checked the connections between the sensors and the Epsilon Internee. He fumbled for a small black box, gripping the lever adorning the top. He studied the Internee's face as he pulled the lever and left it engaged.

The Internee jerked violently, shaking her head to the side and groaning. When she raised her eyes to Pinnacle Officer Cerberus, they were no longer afraid. A cold light gleamed from within, a wry smirk crossing her features.

"How does it feel?"

"I feel... strong. Hungry." She panted, strands of hair sticking to her forehead. "Tell me what to do! I wish to... I wish to fight! To be venerated! Instruct me and I will do as you say."

Pinnacle Officer Cerberus nodded, scrawling a list to record the results.

*Frequency: 450 MHz*

*Adrenaline: 85% increase*

*Aggressiveness: 89% increase*

*Suggestibility: marked increase*

"This is a test. Do you know how to do a test?"

The Internee clenched her fists, pulling the restraints to one side. "Know tests. Do tests all the time. Go! Test me!"

She snarled, tearing at the restraints.

"Say the requital."

The Internee grunted in annoyance. Pinnacle Officer Cerberus unclipped the sensors from the Internee's head.

"We are gathered here to send our gratitude to Pinnacle Officer..." she narrowed her eyes and smiled, baring her teeth. "...Cerberus and FERTS, for our daily provision and protection from those who would seek to strike against our Vassals, our Fighters and our Internees."

"Good. Now, I will give you a challenge. Some transgressors perhaps... yes... perhaps some rogues have breached the ward zone perimeter. They have come to take you away from the provision and protection of FERTS. What do you do?"

The Internee grunted once more, attempting to kick her leg from the restraints.

"I would take this dagger... a small thing, easily concealed, from the Epsilon weapons room. I would wait until they led me away, then when their back was turned, I would expire them. One by one. And I would smile and laugh because they were foolish enough to dare to take us from the safety of FERTS."

"And what would you do, say, if one of these rogues made an attempt, a move to expire the Pinnacle Officer himself?"

The Internee growled, eyes flashing. "I would expire them." She spoke in a low voice, rough at the edges. "I must protect the Pinnacle Officer. I must protect you."

"You know I can't just believe you, not without some kind of proof of your gratitude."

The Internee shifted once more, kicking her legs at the firmly secured restraints.

"I have another test for you. Are you ready?"

"Ready! Yes ready. Go. Test me. Now!"

Pinnacle Officer Cerberus removed the restraints, his hands deftly loosening the leather straps, flicking open the buckles. The Internee leapt from her chair, crouched in Fighter pose, eyes darting around the room.

Pinnacle Officer Cerberus lifted a double pointed spear from the corner of the room, turning to face the fighting creature. It snarled, baring jagged, sharpened teeth. Pinnacle Officer Cerberus flicked the restraint at the end of the chain with the double pointed spear, stepping back as the chain fell away.

The creature launched itself from its spot on the ground, charging towards Pinnacle Officer Cerberus with its jaws opened in a snarling smile.

Pinnacle Officer Cerberus raised the double pointed spear as the creature hurled towards him.

The Internee sprang from her position, sliding under the creature, dragging the knife through its soft underbelly, entrails gushing down over her undershirt. She secured the creature under her arm, deftly slitting its throat and removing the head, tossing it in a corner.

Pinnacle Officer Cerberus set aside the double pointed spear to continue his notes.

The Internee sat in the middle of the room clutching the fighting creature in her lap, face bathed in blood, white teeth flashing in a satisfied, beaming smile. The whites of her eyes peered out from the dark stain of the creature's blood as she petted the creature's hide.

"Good." Pinnacle Officer Cerberus grinned, barely looking up from his notes as he scrawled.

*On conclusion of test, send test subject to Zeta Circuit, effective immediately.*

"Good." He switched off the machine from its 450 MHz position. The Internee slumped, her head lolling to the side.

The Internee blinked, looking up, a confused expression on her face. She looked down at her hands at the blood, the headless fighting creature in her lap. "What..." Her eyes blinked, searching the face of Pinnacle Officer Cerberus for answers that never came. Tears began to fall, washing the blood from her cheeks in streaks. "What have I done?" she whispered, smearing her thighs as she attempted to remove the creature's blood from her hands.

"What have I done?"

# 24

Smoke from the nearby cabins drifted through the air of the camp, along with the lingering scent of cooked potatoes and corn. A pair of sheep bleated in the paddock behind the weapons store. The air was crisp tonight, tinged with the faint scent of rain.

Jotha rubbed his arms, watching his breath turn to fog in the night air. The bone whistle bounced against his chest as he walked from one end of the platform to the other. The moon was a sliver, limiting visibility. He shrugged his shoulders, pacing back and forth in the wooden lookout tower. He rubbed his hands together, wishing for the comfort and warmth of his own bed.

Lookout duty is not to be taken lightly, he thought to himself. You know this.

Rafaella had been on watch the night before, Petra and then Caltha the night before that. It was merely his turn, despite the fact that he had chanced on the coldest night this week. Still, another night of discomfort and he would be back in the warmth of his cabin. He kept himself occupied by imagining the well-stoked fire in his cabin, warmth radiating against the wooden walls, a warming mug of tea in his hands. Just one night, he thought to himself. One more night and I will be comfortable once more. He thought of Liam and Petra, asleep in their beds, blankets pulled up to their chins.

He blew out a breath, watching the cloud of moisture dissipate in front of his face. The tip of his nose was cold to the touch.

Stop your complaining, he thought to himself. You've done this before and you will do it again. It's not as bad as that night it snowed and half the tower roof collapsed on your shoulder. This is nothing. You're being ridiculous.

But something was different tonight, he thought. It was not a real sense, nothing tangible, yet it was there. A *feeling*, a hunch that something was different this time, that something was not right. He listened for any unusual sounds but heard nothing out of the ordinary.

He kept his mind occupied, recalling the first time Rafaella taught him to differentiate between the various sounds and how to isolate the important ones from the usual background noise. He had thought at first that the camp would be a quiet place to sleep as it was a secluded, isolated location with few disturbances. It was only when he began to train his ears to recognize the subtle scurrying of animal activity, the random snapping of branches and the sounds of the wind and rain that he understood the complexity of his task. It was important to listen for all the sounds, including those that were pertinent to the usual activity of the camp, and those that differed from the usual parameters of activity.

Rafaella had taught him to keep his ears and mind open when it came to the sounds and scents of the camp. He scanned the entrance, detecting no movement, as usual. Still, it didn't help to ignore the obvious. He reminded himself to be methodical in his observations. It was true that the camp was protected in part by isolation. It was a comfortable distance away, far from any of the townships. The cliffs provided a natural barrier against intruders, of which there were few, if any. He could recall only two attacks on the camp in total, neither of which had ended well.

He shook his head, willing himself to stop dwelling on the times that had been difficult for them. Life at the camp was good, and as the town liaison, he had the added benefit of procuring supplies for the rest of the camp by posing as a Resident Citizen. His disguise was so well practised that sometimes he found it difficult to remember that he was not a Resident Citizen on a journey for supplies but an intruder, and that the dangers of his each of his journeys were real and would never diminish. The task had fallen to him as Kap and Vern were known by sight to some of the older inhabitants of the townships. They could not risk being recognized in order to procure a few sacks of supplies for the general running of the camp. Liam was far too young to be making the journey on his own and an unaccompanied Sire would draw unwanted attention. As for Rafaella, Caltha, Petra, Bonni and Ginny... well that particular possibility was out of the question. It seemed that Jotha was the only logical choice and he had agreed, reluctantly to put himself at risk. He contented himself with forming connections with the blacksmiths, the wool merchants and those who grew their own crops for trade.

Jotha thought of their latest batch of cattail spirits, grimacing at the memory of the unmistakable taste. Surely there had to be a way to make the spirits more palatable, or at least to stop it stripping the lining of his throat each time he took a sip. He had suggested the idea to Caltha who put forward the idea of strawberries to mask the taste. The idea had some merit, he thought. Anything to get rid of the bitterness of the...

A foreign scent reached his nostrils.

He was used to the familiar smell of the wood fires in the cabins, most of which would have been coals by now. This scent was different. A wilder, almost minty fragrance. He also noted that it was coming from the wrong direction. Jotha scanned the back of the camp, attempting to make out the shapes of the few unoccupied cabins that stood shrouded in darkness.

Never leave your post, he thought to himself. He remembered the words from when Rafaella had first spoken them on his initial attempt at watch duty. But this, this time it was different. The urge to investigate was strong and there was no time to rouse the others. He felt the need to go right now to find the origin of the strange disturbance. He descended the ladder, his feet already in motion as he reached the base of the wooden tower. The scent was coming from the back of the camp, near the overhanging cliffs.

Something did not feel right. The feeling was strong and he knew this feeling well. It was the same feeling he had when an Officer had looked at him once in the township of Evergreen, that hard, calculating gaze boring into him. It was the feeling he had when the mercenaries had ridden from parts unknown. The day they had taken Renn. He would never forget, but Caltha... he was certain there was a part of her that would never recover. Adira was too young to understand that her father was gone, but there would be a part of her that would always remember the feeling of loss. These feelings flowed through him as he picked up speed, heading towards the back of the camp.

Something was wrong. Something was very wrong and he had to find out what it was before he lost the scent. There was an urgency, a desperate push towards his goal. He thought of his post, left unattended in his haste. Rafaella would be furious with him but he had to know. This was important.

He passed the weapons store and the empty cabins, their windows darkened for lack of a fire. He stumbled, almost losing his footing in the dim light of the slivered moon. He scrambled, gripping a branch as he weaved his way through the underbrush to come to the foliage at the base of the cliffs. Smoke began to drift up to his right. He turned, making his way across fallen rocks and pebbles to find the source of the disturbance.

A fire had started up in the leaves of a small shadbush, its white flowers wilting and floating to the ground in droplets of flame. The scent was stronger here, the smell reminding him of burnt berries and scorched fruit. He stamped on the bush, extinguishing the small pockets of flame springing up from the ground.

Something crunched beneath his feet. He lifted his foot to find the broken remains of a large lump of coal. No, not coal, he corrected himself. It was an *ember*.

Jotha ran, his bird-call whistle clamped between his lips. The sound squeaked out, its power thinned by his breathlessness.

He followed the path to the main cabin to find Rafaella and Caltha standing in the doorway, their silhouettes standing out against the warm light within.

"Come inside." Rafaella motioned through the open door.

Jotha rushed through the opening, pausing to rest beside the fire, his hands resting on his knees as he panted. He crouched, warming his hands by the fire as he gasped for another breath.

"An ember... someone lit a fire at the back of the camp. Caught a shadbush, whole thing nearly went up."

"Is it out?" asked Rafaella, fastening her tunic and sheathing her saber. Caltha loaded a bolt into her crossbow, taking extra care not to pull it back to the armed position. She rested it on the table, pointing it to the wall just to be sure. She pulled a warmer woolen tunic over herself, wrapping a belt around her waist.

Jotha looked up at Rafaella. "I got it, the ember's out. Something's not right tonight, Raf. We have to go and check it to make sure. These embers can start up again. It was only small, just one ember, but there may be more."

Rafaella and Caltha shared a look.

Rafaella bent down, placing a hand on his shoulder. "Jotha, I want you to get the others assembled here. No more whistles, no more sounds of any kind if you can help it. Get someone else up on watch, maybe Kap or Vern. I want you here when I talk to the others."

"What do you think it is?" asked Jotha.

"I think we've got company," said Rafaella.

The small group assembled at the main cabin, huddled around a wooden table. The fire smoked away in the hearth, its flames extinguished. Kap had been placed on watch duty, much to his annoyance at being left out of the action. Rafaella had promised to fill him in later, before morning light.

"First off, Lina, I want you to get all the Zeta Internees, Adira and the ones who can't fight, that includes you, 292." Rafaella looked over at 292, the Vassal Jotha had found near the township of Evergreen on one of his supply runs.

292 scowled at her, folding her arms. "Again I do not get to fight. Why?"

"You're not ready, 292. You'll fight when you're ready and not before then. That's final."

"I have trained..."

"Yes, you have trained, but this isn't the same thing. You will watch, and observe as much as you can. Think of it as a test. You won't be doing this without first understanding how it works."

"Fine," 292 said. "I will watch. Observe."

"Good. Now, as I was saying, Lina, you get all of them secured in your cabin and do not, I repeat, do not open that door unless I say so. Got it?"

"Got it," said Lina. Her white hair was illuminated by the fire, her forehead creased in concern. "Are we to arm ourselves? In case..."

"Yes. Always. But nobody gets in, nobody comes out. That is non-negotiable," said Rafaella, spreading a crudely-drawn map of the camp on the table and weighing down the edges with rocks.

"This is different to the last time," said Rafaella. She looked over at Liam, her eyes softening as he gave her a thin smile. "We have to remember this, all of us."

She looked up from the map, scanning the faces of those who had fought beside her in the past. The faces of those who would do so again without hesitation.

She clenched her fist, eyes returning to the map. "Look, it's not just one of us at risk if this goes wrong. If we screw this up, it's Adira, Lina, 292 and Zeta Circuit as well."

Caltha sucked in a breath at the mention of Adira. Rafaella looked up, meeting her eyes. She tried to convey something, a reassurance that this was not as bad as it sounded. The look on Caltha's face said otherwise. Caltha squeezed her eyes shut. She opened her eyes again, giving a brief nod in Rafaella's direction and turning her attention back to the map.

"We split into two groups. I'll be leading the first group, Jotha, you lead the second." Rafaella pointed to the map, tapping at the positions with her finger.

"No," said Caltha.

"What do you mean, *no?*" asked Rafaella.

"I will lead the second group."

"No, Cal," said Rafaella. "You know we're better as a team. It's the way we've always done things."

"Well, not this time. It's Adira this time. I have to be out there. If something happened..."

Rafaella said nothing, placing a hand on Caltha's shoulder. The memory of Adira's father hung in the silence that followed. The reminders of Renn had never left the camp and it was accepted that this was a topic not to be discussed. It was not a new memory, but it would never be forgotten. Rafaella nodded in understanding. If Adira was taken, if her last remaining parent failed to keep her safe, Caltha would never forgive herself. As much as she disagreed, she understood Caltha's reasoning.

"Fine," she said, clenching her jaw. "Okay, that's settled then. Caltha, you lead the second group." Rafaella looked back to the map. "What do we know so far?"

"Not much," said Jotha. "There's someone out there but I can't be sure how many. Most likely above the cliffs, I'm guessing not too far from the edge."

Rafaella glanced at the coals smoking in the hearth, a line forming between her brows.

"All of this seems wrong," said Jotha. "I have a strange feeling about it. Nobody builds a fire on the edge of a cliff, it just wouldn't make sense. So what were they doing up there?" The only response was silence.

Rafaella ran a hand over her face, leaning back from the table. "Someone wanted us to know."

Jotha nodded. "That must be it. It's what I thought when I first saw it. It's unlikely anyone dropped an ember over the edge by accident."

"So, what? We're dealing with a group? Mercenaries? Someone wanted to get our attention. Maybe someone who isn't there by choice." Rafaella blew out a breath, tapping a location on the map. "It came from here. Follow that line for long enough and you come to the river. Follow the river far enough and you come to... well, I don't get the feeling they came from one of the townships. Someone tracked us down, they know we're here. That leads me to believe we're dealing with FERTS. I don't have any proof of this, but think about it. We came to them, we took Zeta Circuit out from under their noses." Rafaella cursed under her breath. "I don't know how, but they found us."

"FERTS? But how?" asked Petra. "We were careful. We covered our tracks well, I'm sure of it."

"Not well enough," said Rafaella. "It doesn't matter now, it's done. We don't have a choice anymore. I don't know how they found us, but we do know one thing. Someone gave us a warning and I intend to use it. Let's take it that whoever this was, they were telling us to plan for an attack. I'm guessing that this attack is likely to happen tomorrow. Why else would it come tonight?"

"We don't know that, Raf," said Bonni. "It could mean anything."

"Yeah it could. It could mean anything, it could mean nothing, but we're not taking any chances. Synchronize your timepieces, we do this before first light. Kap, get the animals secured and out of the way. We don't want any distractions. Everyone puts their cabin fires out tonight. No exceptions. I don't care how cold it is. Got it?"

The group nodded, glancing around at each other.

"We don't know much, Raf," said Vern.

"No, we don't know, that's the problem. But it's all we've got to go on. If we're ready and nothing comes of it, it's better than the other way around."

"What if it really is nothing?" asked Ginny.

"It it's nothing, we should consider ourselves lucky. But I don't think it is. Liam?" Liam looked up from the map, wide eyed. "You did well last time, even though I know it was hard for you to see what you saw once we got there. It was a lot to take in." Rafaella studied his face. "Look, I won't ask you for something you don't want to do, but I think you've proved yourself to be ready. That is, if you think you're ready for it. It's dangerous, I won't pretend otherwise."

"Liam, wait. Whatever it is, you don't have to do this." Petra stepped forward, putting a hand on Liam's shoulder. She leaned in between Liam and Rafaella, face grim. "Raf, come on," she whispered. "He's too young for this, you know that. Find someone else."

"No," said Rafaella. "This won't work if we use someone who looks like they might be a real threat. No offence, Liam."

He looked up at Petra, patting her hand and shaking his head. He cleared his throat to speak. "No, it's okay. I'm ready. Whatever it is, I want to do it."

Rafaella smiled, eyes crinkling at the corners. "Okay. Okay, that's good. See here?" She pointed to a spot on the map, tapping her finger and motioning for Liam to come closer. "Group one will be covering you. I won't let you out of my sight, just remember that. If they've got crossbows or anything like that I want you out of there fast, no exceptions. That's an order."

Liam nodded, focusing his eyes on the map.

"Now listen carefully," said Rafaella, pointing to a spot on the map. "This is where we begin..."

# 25

At first light Officer Tor began the FERTS requital, the Epsilon Internees answering in unison. 201 remained silent, mouthing the words.

"We send our gratitude to Pinnacle Officer Cerberus and FERTS."

As the dutiful reply came, 201 caught the sight of High Training Room Officer Reno's eyes, a cold glint residing within their depths. She furrowed her brow. He would not look at her, eyes scanning the rest of the Epsilon Fighters, making the necessary preparations. The weapons were hooked around his shoulder, bundled together in a wide leather casing. The shields lay at the ready, lined around the inside of the cart. As the Epsilon Fighters passed by 201, the words of the FERTS requital fresh in their minds, the only words that came to 201 were those words spoken by an unknown voice, the instructions handed in secret, the scroll tightly bound.

*Destroy it. Destroy it all.*

Something about the words did not fit her understanding. The words were clear, their meaning unmistakable, yet they made no sense to her. 201 watched Reno, looking for a sign that he would do as instructed. Reno was an Officer, one who was used to following orders, she thought. This was all she needed to know. She would find no answers from Reno himself.

The Epsilon Fighters were dressed in full battle regalia. Their feet marched by, sheathed in cris-crossed bound leather. The Fighters wore leather breastplates, their finely muscled arms clenched around ornate leather shields. Their leather skirts were high and impractical, more suited to the theatrics of the Epsilon Games ring than an actual battle situation. 201 watched them pass, noting details of their armor, the way the stitching was joined at the sides, anything to take her mind off the ensuing battle.

What do I know of battle, she thought. I am merely a trainee, suited for weapons duty.

The battle armor was taken, one for each Epsilon Fighter, leaving only 201 to prepare for battle in her soiled Omega jumpsuit. She looked down at the material, running it through her fingers. The jumpsuit would offer no protection against the onslaught of the elements, let alone the tip of a weapon.

*I will surely be expired today, but I will not be expired within those walls.*

As the Epsilon Fighters stepped into the cage, Reno handed each of them their weapon of choice, nodding as they passed. When 201 moved to enter the cart Reno stopped her with his elbow. He handed over a spare spatha. Her chosen weapon, the bastard sword, had been handed out to another Epsilon Fighter, presumably one more deserving of such a weapon. 201 wondered if this was a sign that she would not be fortunate in this battle. She snorted, attempting a smile.

"Stay to the back of the group, 201," said Reno. "You're not a Fighter yet. Don't forget that."

201 nodded, ducking her head to enter the cart for the last part of their journey.

She sat back against the bars, jolting from side to side as the horses began to lurch ahead. She heard Reno flick the reins as the cart began to pick up speed along the beginnings of a path.

"What did Reno say to you?" 299 sat in the corner at the opposite end of the cart, her dark green eyes unwavering, fixed on 201's face.

"He told me to stay at the back of the group," 201 said.

"Perhaps he does not want you to be hurt? How sweet of our High Training Room Officer to do such a thing. Though I don't see why. Your face is already a mess, a good fight would hardly make a difference."

201 stared back at 299. "No, that is not why. He said I was not a Fighter yet. That is why I must not be at the front of the group."

"Well he's right, of course. That is exactly why I will lead. You are not a Fighter." 299 grimaced at her. "You will never be a Fighter. You are nothing but a lowly weapons duty Internee. You have not tasted the adulation of the Epsilon Games ring like I have. You do not know what it is to earn the glory of FERTS."

"I do not wish to, either," said 201.

"How dare you speak of..."

"I do hope you are fortunate today, 299." 201 adjusted her spatha to fit it between her feet.

"I have my chosen weapon." 299 patted the blade of her scimitar, pricking her finger on the sharpened point and licking the blood from her fingertip. She grinned at 201, leaning back against the bars.

"Well then." 201 smiled, her eyes crinkling at the corners. "You are truly lucky."

The cart wound its way down the incline, doubling back towards the camp. The cart passed through shadowed caves, winding through a grove encasing a magnificent waterfall surrounded by smooth rocks carpeted in a thick covering of moss. 201 stared at the waterfall through the bars, mesmerized by the constant flow of the water rushing over rocks, splashing against moss amongst a beautiful array of wildflowers, sending a plume of sweet-smelling mist rising into the air.

The horses slowed to a tentative pace as they approached through the valley, nearing the entrance that would take them to their destination.

*This is it. The camp.*

Twin cliffs loomed above them. The formations arched towards each other as if reaching out but never quite making contact. Vast, curved shadows from the archway fell over their cart, blocking out the distant heat from the first light of the morning sun.

*Akecheta.*

201 clenched her spatha, knuckles turning white against the hilt. This was not how it was supposed to end.

299 looked over at 201. "Don't tell me you are afraid, 201." She laughed, shaking her head.

201 raised her eyes to 299, her gaze piercing through her. "Yes. I am afraid. Of course I am afraid." She raised an eyebrow at 299. "Aren't you?"

"I am not afraid. I am an Epsilon Fighter. I have earned the adulation of FERTS many times over. My achievements are venerated, and I have never failed to be victorious." 299 chuckled. "No, I am not afraid."

"You should be," said 201, staring through 299.

"Do not listen to her, 299," said 263. "She is just jealous that she did not get her chosen weapon. Or a shield."

"Or armor," said 277. The Epsilon Fighters broke into laughter.

"Quiet," called Reno, pummeling his fist on the front of the cage.

"Even now, he wishes to protect you," muttered 299. "I do not understand. You're not so pretty now, I made sure of that."

"You do not understand," said 201. "He told you... he told *us* to be quiet so our approach will not be detected by the camp's inhabitants," said 201. "Do you wish to alert them to our presence, 299? No, I would think not."

299 stared at her scimitar, scratching her fingernail against the hilt. For once, 299 and the rest of the Epsilon Fighters were silent.

The fighting creature lay secured in the carriage near Officer Tor's boots, the leash pulled tightly around its neck. It rested, lulled by the movement of the cart wheels as they bounced along the dirt trail.

201 watched, her heart beating faster as they ventured through the archway of the twin cliffs. A shadow fell across her face. She squeezed her eyes shut, trying to visualize the symbol in her mind.

*Please. Please help me. Tell me what to do.*

There was no answer.

The camp appeared deserted. No fires burned and no smoke rose from the chimneys of the various cabins dotted throughout the camp.

The cart squeaked along the trail. Reno slowed the horses to a tentative shuffle, their hoofbeats softening on the damp ground to hide their approach.

Reno turned to Officer Tor, fixing him with a pointed look.

"I will go in first. When we reach the entrance, do as I do. Say as I say, and do not make any decisions of your own accord. Do you understand?"

"I will follow your lead, Sir."

"No sudden movements, this is a serious matter. You are clear on this?"

"I am clear, yes. You have my word."

Reno stopped the horses, handing the reins to Officer Tor.

"Keep your eyes open."

Officer Tor nodded, gripping the reins, flicking them for the horses to proceed. The horses trotted, pulled back by Tor's hold on the reins, hoofs landing on the uneven ground, the clicks sounding out of time.

Reno strode before the cart, broadening the gap between himself and the horses. He unsheathed his spatha, adjusting his grip as he walked.

Reno walked alone, his arms hanging loose by his sides. His black shirt was unfastened at the neck, untucked from his dark trousers. Sweat beaded at his temples but his face remained impassive.

He sniffed the air, catching scent of something unfamiliar, a sweet, fragrant scent, bright and vibrant. No signs of activity emanated from the cabins and the fields were deserted, bathed in silence.

He stood on the path at the heart of the camp, noting the tracks winding in all directions, leading to each of the cabins. The sound of his boots scuffed across the dirt path. Still, he heard nothing. Turning in a slow circle, he took in his surroundings, taking a deep breath.

201 watched Reno's movements. He seemed to follow no discernible pattern.

*What are you doing, Reno? Do you feel nothing?*

She gripped the bars, leaning forward. 299 jabbed her in the side with the handle of her scimitar. 299 narrowed her eyes at 201, a warning for her not to make a move.

201 scanned the camp for any signs of movement but the camp seemed empty. There were no sounds, nothing to indicate any type of activity.

But the camp did not *feel* empty. She could feel the essence of the camp's inhabitants seeping out through the path and winding its way to her through the bars.

Reno turned to face them, a brief gesture of his hand signaling for them to follow. It was clear that Reno had not sensed anything approaching what 201 had felt. She felt her face growing cold, a tingle beginning to make its way up her spine.

201 lurched to the side, arms and elbows pushing against her as the Epsilon Fighters filed out, their sheathed weapons clicking against the door of the cage. The group moved forward, stepping in an orderly line, eyes darting to the front and sides. 201 took a deep breath, pushing herself through the door of the cart to land on the soft ground, glancing around for a possible route of escape. She caught the eye of Officer Tor at the helm. He stood, grinning at her, unraveling the leash for the fighting creature. The creature showed its teeth, its gold-tinged eyes following her movements as she unsheathed her spatha, following at the rear of the group of Epsilon Fighters.

She had no armor or shield, feeling exposed as she stepped up her pace to catch up with the group, eyes darting to the sides once more for a possible escape route. She stepped forward, bumping into 263 as the group halted. The Epsilon Fighters at the head of the group had hesitated, their figures standing motionless. 201 looked ahead, trying to catch sight of what had caused them to stop. She edged forward, making her way through the group, attempting to see what had caught their attention.

She felt a chill when she saw the first signs of movement.

A figure appeared at the end of the path. He was young, perhaps only 15Y or so, and unarmed.

*Liam.*

His light hair hung over his ears and his blue eyes squinted in the morning mist. He walked with the enthusiastic, yet uncoordinated gait of one who has not yet fully grown into their body. He stopped when he spotted the group of Epsilon Fighters, his boots skidding, digging into the ground. His eyes widened as he stepped backwards, turning to run.

*Liam. No!*

"Get him!" cried 299, charging forward. 201's heart sped up, her adrenaline surging as 263 followed with a shout, bringing the rest of the Epsilon Fighters along with her. 201 was caught in the rush of bodies, leather and shields bumping against her, knocking her off-balance.

201 kicked and struggled, covering her head with her arms and crouching low to the ground. She pulled her limbs in towards herself, curling her body to make herself as small as possible. The Epsilon Fighters surged forward, boots trampling the ground, their cries echoing against the cliffs.

201 lifted her head, fingers digging into the ground as she pushed herself into Fighter pose, her knees bent into a crouch. She watched as the Epsilon Fighters charged, heading for the lone figure.

The figure stopped, turning to face them, a whistle jutting out from between his lips.

His cheeks puffed out in a strong, steady exhale, his cheeks flushing with the effort. The sound, shrill and piercing, broke through the quiet of the morning, reverberating throughout the valley. It sounded like a bird, a night bird call perhaps, but this was no bird, it was a warning.

*A signal. The signal.*

"No!" Reno shouted.

299 and the Epsilon Fighters chased Liam over the rise at the end of the path. He was unarmed, his small form helpless against the oncoming group. He looked up at the approaching Epsilon Fighters, eyes wide and mouth hanging open. He backed away, edging down the path. 299 reached the top, charging down the slope towards the lone figure as 263 and the rest of the Epsilon Fighters fell in behind her.

"No, 299!" Reno called, throwing his arms out but the group was too far from his grasp to be of any use. He turned, swiveling until he was facing 201.

She looked up from her Fighter pose on the path, watching Reno's movements. She bent her knees, ankles flexing.

299 pursued the lone figure, charging down the path on the other side of the rise. "For FERTS!" she cried.

"For FERTS!" came the answering call, the clink of weapons filling the air as the Epsilon Fighters followed her lead.

299 bellowed, raising her scimitar, the weapon that had brought her so much adulation in the Epsilon Games ring. But this was not the Epsilon Games.

Liam stopped, turning on his heel to face them, his face pale, shining with perspiration. He stood, hands shaking at his sides. He stood as they approached, waiting for the Epsilon Fighters with their swords drawn, closing in on his position. Liam screamed, the sound piercing through the valley.

299 skidded down the path, charging towards victory. She ran, dimly aware of a tug at her ankles.

Liam fell to the ground, landing on his knees.

"Now! Now!" he shouted.

A rope pulled taut at the level of their feet, strong hands on either side of the tree tugging to hold the rope firmly in place. The Epsilon Fighters stumbled against each other, grappling for purchase.

299 found herself falling, twisting, tangled, her scimitar rising up towards her own face. She pushed it away, her hands hooking upwards as she tumbled to the ground. There was a flapping sound from above. 299 flung her head from side to side but still she could not determine the origin of the noise.

A blanket of ropes snapped down from the trees, the weight snagging 263's trident and dragging the Epsilon Fighters, pinning them to the ground.

263 called out, attempting to unhook her weapon only to find it was snagged in the netting. She looked up to see a rough hand, reddened from the sun. The hand grasped the trident, pulling it through the rope netting. 263 groaned as the weapon dislodged from her fingers, tugged away from her grip and out of reach. She smacked at the ground, hands grasping at nothing.

275 roared in confusion, springing from a tangle of ropes, spatha at the ready as she crouched in

Fighter pose. She halted as a finely honed metal tip gleamed in her field of vision, the point almost touching her nose. As her eyes unblurred, the wooden frame of Caltha's crossbow sharpened into focus along with a pair of blue eyes staring down at her.

275 raised her open hand towards Caltha's crossbow, the other hand lowering her weapon to the ground.

"Don't move. I mean it," said Caltha. "Stay where you are."

275 kept her hands in the air, her eyes tracking the inhabitants filtering out from their concealment and securing the Epsilon Fighters underneath the ropes. Caltha raised a hand to signal two of the others. They approached to gather weapons, collecting, stacking shields and checking for any concealed threats.

"Make sure you get all their weapons," she said, looking down at 275. "You're not going to give me any trouble are you?" 275 shook her head.

263 edged towards her, hands outstretched towards their captors. 277 remained still but 275 was restless.

"I said don't move, are we clear?" Caltha's eyes narrowed, focusing on 263.

"We will not give you trouble," said 263, raising her hands in placation. She caught 275's eye, shooting her a warning look.

299 watched the proceedings with a practised eye, waiting until the group turned towards the dark haired one for instruction. 299 sized her up. The dark haired one was shorter than the others, though they

seemed to listen to her, following her instructions without question. Though it made no sense, it seemed that she was one of the leaders. A fitting target, she decided. She watched as the short one pointed to the end of the rope, loosely wound around the base of a tree.

"Get that end, it's coming loose," said Caltha.

299 took the opportunity to slide the dagger from her boot, slicing through the ropes holding her down.

She sprang from her position, launching herself towards the dark haired figure. She grunted in satisfaction as her dagger connected with flesh, plunging to the hilt. Caltha fell on her back, the wind knocked out of her. 299 smiled, revealing the look that had made her the most feared Fighter in Epsilon Circuit. Caltha's eyes widened, her mouth open in shock.

299 lunged forward again, gasping in a breath as something hard and cold entered her chest. It sliced through her, chilling her blood. She staggered back, the bloodied dagger falling from her hand.

She looked down at her pierced leather breastplate, watching in confusion as blood gushed from her wound, the polished wooden bolt protruding from her chest. She fell to the ground, blood soaking into the earth beneath her, hands twitching in the air.

Caltha lay, her back pressed to the base of a tree, her weapon angled towards the spot where 299 had once stood, its load discharged.

She scrabbled back with her feet, edging herself to an upright position. She fumbled with a new bolt, fingers shaking as she loaded the crossbow, swinging it to point at 299's position on the ground.

299 rolled to the side, breath wheezing from her tightly muscled body. Caltha watched her chest rise and fall as she took another rattling breath.

299 coughed, letting out a small laugh.

"We send our gratitude to..." 299 whispered. Her fingers twitched, clenching into a fist. Caltha watched as the fist relaxed, fingers splaying out and becoming still.

"Cal!" Liam ran towards her, whistle swinging from his neck as 205 and 278 and two of the other Epsilon Fighters burst from the hole in the netting, their scimitars and bastard swords swinging through the air.

"Look out!" shouted Caltha. Petra and Ginny rushed from their position near the trees to intercept the Epsilon Fighters as they charged towards Caltha. Petra clashed with 205's scimitar, her saber trembling under the weight. This one was strong, Petra thought. Too strong. She felt herself being pushed to the ground, saber locked above her head.

Ginny leapt through the air, her saber piercing 278's chest. She tumbled to the ground, saber still hooked through a gap in the Epsilon Fighter's leather breastplate. She kicked out with her leg, dislodging her saber and slicing towards another Epsilon Fighter armed with a bastard sword. The bastard sword tumbled to the ground. She looked up to find yet another Epsilon Fighter above her, spatha raised. Ginny raised her eyes to her attacker, waiting for the final blow. The Fighter swung her spatha then stopped, eyes growing wide. She collapsed to the side to reveal Liam kneeling behind her, crossbow resting on his knee, one eye closed.

Petra cried out, the strength in her arms giving way. The scimitar loomed above her, 205's grinning face staring down. Petra fell to the ground on one knee, the scimitar slicing at her arm before she heard the thud of her opponent's body hitting the ground. She raised her head to see Caltha bleeding on the ground, wedged against the base of a tree, her crossbow pointing at 205's former position.

"You did well today, Liam," said Caltha, her voice thick with fatigue. She leaned back on her elbow. "Yeah, you did good," she whispered.

Liam put his hand on Caltha's forehead. "We've gotta get Raf."

"No, don't. We stick to the plan." Caltha put a hand on Liam's arm. Petra and Ginny helped Vern secure 263, 277 and 275 under ropes.

Reno and 201 listened to the cries as they rang out, the clash of metal on metal echoing through the valley. A piercing howl sounded out before everything became still.

"Fools, all of them." Reno shook his head. "299," he muttered to himself.

201 flexed her ankles, springing upright, eyes locked with Reno, watching for his next move. Reno looked at her in confusion. His eyes widened as a crossbow bolt pierced the ground at his feet.

201 took the opportunity to grab Reno's spatha, hitting the hilt of her own sword on his wrist until he released his grip.

"201, what are you doing?"

201 dropped her spatha, kicking it out of reach. She grabbed Reno's hands. Reno shook her off, sweeping out his leg to kick at 201's ankles, toppling them to the ground. 201 hooked her leg around Reno's as he reached for his spatha.

"Answer me, 201! What are you doing?"

"Quiet!" she said. She leaned closer to Reno, whispering in his ear. "I am saving you from being expired. Listen to me, Reno. Say nothing and do as I do, and nothing more. We are outnumbered, you must trust me on this. Do as I do."

201 released Reno's hands, raising her own hands in the air. Reno watched, eyes darting to the side, mirroring her movements.

"We will not fight!" called 201. "We have no weapons!" She pushed Reno's elbow, urging him to stand. "We will not fight you!"

A low voice rang out, echoing around them. It was fierce, yet warm. The voice was strangely familiar to 201's ears.

"You came here armed," said the voice.

201 froze.

"You came here to fight us," the voice said. "Now you have found us, I cannot let you leave."

201 squinted, resting her hands on her head. She swiveled her head to the left, then to the right. She focused her eyes on a particular tree to her right but

she could not see through the leaves to find the origin of the voice, though she was sure she had found the right one. She slowed her breathing, hissing through her teeth to calm herself.

"Please. We will not fight," she said, attempting to keep her voice calm and her breaths steady.

"Don't move," said the voice. "I'll shoot if you move."

201 closed her eyes, picturing dirty blonde hair woven into a plait, greenish-brown eyes crinkling at the corners.

201's eyes widened. "Raf?"

"How did you..." There was a rustling in the leaves. "Only my friends call me Raf."

"Please..." said 201. "Please Raf... Rafaella. Do not harm us."

201 felt a presence behind her, hands grasping her own, securing them with rope. Reno stared at her, flinching as the ropes wound around his own wrists.

"Don't move," said a voice behind her. She nodded at Reno, signaling for him to remain still. Reno narrowed his eyes, glaring at 201.

"He said don't move. I suggest you listen," said the voice.

"We will not fight you," 201 repeated. "Please."

"How did you know my name?" asked the voice.

"Yes, 201," Reno whispered through his teeth. "How did you know her name? I would also like to know the answer to this question."

201 thought quickly, a cold sweat forming on her back. "I have heard of you. They say you are a great leader."

"Do not be foolish, 201," whispered Reno. "Everyone knows that a Vassal cannot lead..."

A branch snapped, sending a twig floating down from above. A pair of leather boots came into view, followed by legs encased in leather pants. Then a dark tunic, a blonde plait swinging across her shoulder as she alighted from the tree, a crossbow in one hand. She dropped to the ground, standing before them. She stood taller than 201, eyes darting to Reno and back to 201, assessing which of them would pose the greatest threat.

"They were carrying these," said the one holding Reno's wrists behind his back. Rafaella bent down to pick up one of the spathas, never lowering her gaze from Reno and 201. She flipped the spatha over in her hand. She raised an eyebrow at Reno.

"Nice. Where are the others?"

Officer Tor struggled against the ropes binding his arms. He smirked, fingers loosening on the fighting creature's leash. Voices came from further up the path, growing louder as they approached. The rest of the camp's inhabitants came over the rise, dragging the rope-bound 263, 277 and 275 along with them.

"This is all of them?" Rafaella glanced at the three newcomers.

Liam arrived, out of breath. "We tried to get them to surrender, but they wouldn't listen. The big one, with the red hair. She hurt..."

Rafaella spotted Caltha staggering from the trees, hands gripping the bark to steady herself.

"Cal!" Rafaella rushed to Caltha's side. Caltha wheezed, lowering herself to the ground. Rafaella touched her face, her arms, checking for wounds. She stopped, peeling back the layers of Caltha's tunic, revealing a dark stain.

"Get Lina! Now!" Rafaella shouted, signaling to one of the outer cabins. The door burst open to reveal a small group led by a tall figure with white hair.

"Ma!" 201 watched as a little one ran from the cabin, ducking the hands that reached to grasp her tunic and keep her inside. She broke free, heading towards Rafaella and Caltha who sat huddled together on the ground.

Officer Tor stood behind at a distance, a saber pointed at his back, the fighting creature snarling at the end of the leash. The creature spotted Adira, its gold-tinted eyes locking in on her tiny form as she stumbled towards Caltha. The creature snarled, jaws snapping against the leash.

It jolted ahead, sending Officer Tor stumbling back against the saber. He arched his back against the sting of the blade, the creature releasing from his grip and charging towards Adira.

201 clenched her hands, unable to move as the sharpened jaws flew towards Adira, snapping and growling. Adira screamed.

"Break! Break!" shouted Reno, but the creature paid no attention.

The creature sailed in the air, landing and twitching at Rafaella's feet. It squirmed on the ground, claws digging into the dirt, a stream of blood staining the grass beneath its midsection. The jaws opened and closed, snapping at nothing. Rafaella held the crossbow at eye level, breathing rapidly. She lowered the crossbow, loading another bolt and pointing it towards the creature.

Adira stood still, staring at the mouth of the creature. Its jaw twitched, falling open on a low whine.

"Adira..." said Caltha.

"Ma!" Adira edged her way to Caltha, cradling her head and patting her hair. "Please, I don't want you to die!"

"Shh, shh." Caltha shrugged her off, attempting a smile. "Who's dying? Nobody is dying." She grabbed Adira's chin. "I'm fine."

Rafaella pulled Caltha to her feet, slinging an arm around her shoulders. "You're not fine," Rafaella whispered. Caltha stopped, turning to Adira.

"I have to go with Lina now. Get back in the cabin and don't come out until Raf says it is safe. I will speak to you later about coming out before it is safe."

"But..."

"No arguing. Go!" Caltha coughed, leaning against Rafaella. Adira ran to the cabin, glancing back at Caltha before disappearing inside. Caltha collapsed, falling against Rafaella's shoulder.

"Come on, come on. Lina!" Rafaella handed Caltha over to Lina. "Go, get her out of here!"

Rafaella turned to face the others. Her face was pinched, her jaw twitching. "Get these two in one of the back cabins." She pointed to 201 and Reno. "And split these four up, two in each cabin. I'll deal with them later."

Rafaella strode towards the main cabin at the front of the camp, unloading her crossbow as she walked.

Reno's mouth remained open, watching the departing figure of Rafaella.

"Come on you two," a voice said behind them. 201 looked back at the lifeless form of the fighting creature as strong hands led them towards the outer cabin. The hands shoved them through the doorway, pushing them down to the straw-covered floor. Their feet were secured with ropes and they were left alone, the door slamming behind them.

# 26

201 leaned against the wooden wall, ropes secured around her wrists and ankles. She looked at the straw covering the floor, the window above her head, the door on the right. She avoided Reno's stare, though she felt it weighing upon her.

"201."

She looked at her feet, wondering if there was some way to release them from the ropes, but they were well-secured. Perhaps, if given enough time...

"201."

She looked up to find Reno staring over at her with a barely-suppressed fury behind his gaze.

"Yes?"

"Do you think..." He gritted his teeth. "Do you think perhaps now is a good time to tell me what you know?"

"What do you mean, Reno? I don't know any more than you do." 201 edged her feet forward, stretching her legs, attempting to make herself more comfortable.

"You're a terrible liar."

"Maybe I am."

"You did this. Somehow, you did this."

"I would think 299 did this, charging after Li... an unarmed opponent."

"299 must be venerated. I will not hear you speaking of 299 in that way."

"I will not venerate 299, and not simply for the reason that she expired 232. I will not venerate her because she enjoyed it."

"Well of course, there is satisfaction in knowing you have done a great service to FERTS, the glory of earning the adulation at the Epsilon Games."

"I will not venerate 299," said 201.

"Why? Because you do not believe it is right to fight?"

201 opened her mouth to speak, closing it again. She twitched, shifting her position to make herself more comfortable. She thought for a moment, studying the ropes around her ankles.

"No. I do not believe it is wrong to fight. But it is the *reason* for the fight that is important. 299 enjoyed it for the love of fighting. I will not venerate 299 for this reason."

"How dare you? 299 was a great champion of the Epsilon Games ring! She gave thanks for her protection, gave thanks to the Pinnacle Officer. You have no right to say what you are saying!"

"Did you know that what one says and what one really thinks are not always the same thing?"

"You speak foolish words, 201. You make no sense."

"I make no sense to one who will not see the meaning. You will understand what you understand.

Every mind is different. A word spoken to one will mean something completely different to the next. Everyone hears what they are willing to accept, and nothing more."

"There you go again, speaking senseless words."

"Those who heard 232 speak in the Epsilon Games ring did not understand. Perhaps I was the only one who heard."

"Enough of this talk. This is unforeseen. And unpleasant," said Reno, struggling to adjust the ropes around his wrists, the skin becoming flushed as he rubbed the ropes against the wall. "Why must our feet be bound as well?"

"I am used to it," said 201, shrugging. "It has not been long since I fell asleep bound to a cart. At least here it is warm, and there is straw."

Reno furrowed his brow, turning away from 201.

"I suppose you will get used to it as well," said 201.

"What do you mean you are used to it? You were not always bound."

"I mean this." She gestured with her head, signaling the space within the cabin. "This here is no different to my confinement at FERTS. Though I will sleep more soundly, knowing who is outside this door. How strange that you, an Officer, should find yourself in such a position."

"Confinement? How dare you speak of FERTS in this way! How dare you speak of the Officers..."

"What is the time?" asked 201.

Reno scowled, twisting his wrists to read his timepiece, craning his neck. "It is no use. I cannot read it."

201 leaned across to read the timepiece. "It is 06:19. Like I said before, at least the straw is warm. We might as well rest before they come for us." 201 edged into the corner, stretching out next to the wall.

"What? You know they will not let us leave, 201. How can you be so calm about this?"

"They will not harm you, Reno." 201 stared up at the ceiling.

"Have you lost your senses? They are mercenaries! They will expire us before the night is over!"

"They are not mercenaries."

"Rogues, mercenaries! Whatever you will call them, they are the enemy! What is important is that they will expire us and send parts of us back to FERTS!"

"Is that what you fear? Strange that it differs so greatly from my fear. A fear you could not understand, even if you wanted to."

"I am your trainer!" Reno shouted. "I advise you. I train you. You do not speak to me about my mind and what it can do. Do you understand?"

201 turned her head to face him. "Did you wonder, Reno, why they did not expire 263, 277, Officer Tor and 275? Or you and me for that matter?"

Reno banged his boots on the ground, leaning back against the wall. His breaths were rapid and his face was red. He shuffled his boots in the straw, calming his breaths. He let out a long exhale, staring up at the roof of the cabin.

"That... that is simple," he said. "They are waiting to question us. When they have the answers they need, they will expire us."

"Like you would have eventually done with me?"

Reno did not reply.

201 took a deep breath, listening to the sounds of birds outside the window of their cabin.

"They did not expire us because they did not need to do so. We gave up our weapons and we are no longer a threat to them." She turned her head in the straw to face Reno. "Had they been mercenaries, or rogues as you called them, we would not be having this conversation. Why are you so convinced they are mercenaries?"

"Because they..."

"Because they what?" 201 narrowed her eyes.

"Everyone knows that mercenaries are the primary threat to FERTS. This is further proof of the need for the strengthening of Vassal protection. It is clear that the Pinnacle Officer has been wise in his decisions."

201 turned her head back to face the ceiling. Her eyes were getting heavy and sleep seemed a welcome respite from the day's activities, though it was barely morning. She closed her eyes, her breathing slowing down. "Did you ever wonder, Reno, why we have not seen a real mercenary in all this time? It was such a long journey, and yet... nothing."

Reno was silent for a time, pondering her words. He watched the morning sun filter through the window, illuminating the straw. He listened to the excited chatter of birds as they flitted about in the trees outside the cabin. The distant hiss of the waterfall soothed his beating heart. He looked over at 201, her form huddled, head resting on the straw as the light fell on her bruised and swollen features.

"201?"

There was no answer, save for the rise and fall of her breath as she drifted to sleep.

# 27

Rafaella burst through the door of the cabin, leaving it banging on its hinges. Caltha lay on blankets near the hearth, the fire still unlit. She was covered in a thin layer of sweat, shivering.

"How did this happen?" Rafaella said. She edged past Lina to Caltha's side, putting a hand to her forehead. "Why is there no fire yet? She's freezing!"

The sun had risen outside, yet the inside of the cabin was chilled from a night without a fire in the hearth. The room stank of boiled cloves, masking the underlying tang of blood and sweat. Rafaella moved away from Caltha to let Lina through with another cloth soaked in the clove mixture. Rafaella hovered, watching Caltha's face as she winced from the sting.

"Cal? Can you hear me?" asked Rafaella. "Hey..."

"That's enough, Raf. I need you to move back," said Lina, pointing a bloodied cloth in her direction.

"That's not going to happen," said Rafaella, eyes never leaving Caltha's form. "Cal? Just blink or something. Please..."

"Raf..." Caltha opened her eyes, trying to focus.

"Shh, you don't have to speak." Rafaella clenched her jaw. "Just... that's good. Lina's going to fix you up, you'll be fine," said Rafaella.

"Yeah, I'm fine." Caltha closed her eyes and laughed, choking on a cough.

Lina elbowed Rafaella out of the way, continuing to bathe Caltha's wounds.

"Raf, I won't ask you again. Get out of here and get me some cloth, some more of the clove mixture from the stove and boil some more hot water." Lina's voice was firm.

Rafaella took one more glance at Caltha and left for the kitchen, banging pots against the wood-fired stove.

Caltha coughed, attempting to speak. "She's..."

"Shh, I know, I know, Cal." Lina smiled down at her. "But she was right about one thing though, it's not a good idea for you to speak." She rolled the material of Caltha's tunic further up her body, her eyes squinting as she caught sight of the wound. "And a knife, Raf!" she called out.

Rafaella appeared in the doorway, carrying cloth and a bowl of clove mixture. She placed it at Lina's feet and returned with a knife, watching as Lina sliced the material to reveal the extent of Caltha's injury.

Rafaella sucked in a breath, the blood draining from her face.

"How is it?" asked Caltha.

"It's not so bad." Rafaella grinned, placing a hand on Caltha's forearm, the smile failing to reach her eyes. "I'll just go get the water, should be boiled by now."

Rafaella disappeared through the doorway. Caltha reached up and gripped at the sleeve of Lina's tunic.

"It's bad, isn't it," said Caltha, lifting her head to look up at Lina.

"Yeah, Cal. It's not good. But you already knew that. Lie back now."

Caltha grimaced, shifting to a more comfortable position. "She was fast for someone so big," she said, blinking to clear her vision. "I didn't expect that. But I got her, Lina."

Lina dipped the cloth in the clove mixture, wringing it out. "I'm going to need you to be quiet now. This is going to hurt, but the cloves will numb it a little. Try and stay still, okay?"

Caltha grimaced, nodding her head.

"Raf?" she called out. "Can you get the fire started?" Rafaella reappeared in the doorway, arms loaded with wood.

"Got it, got it already. What are you waiting for?" She stacked wood in the hearth. "Don't wait for me."

"It's so cold in here, Raf," said Caltha. Rafaella squeezed her eyes shut, breathing out in a rush. She dropped the last log, disappearing back into the kitchen.

"Stay with me, Cal," said Lina. She soaked her hands in the clove mixture, placing both hands on Caltha's chest, prising apart the wound. The blood flow was erratic. It leaked out, slowing to almost nothing before leaking again, adding stripes to the forked pattern trailing down her body.

"She missed your heart," said Lina.

"Are you sure?" said Rafaella, kneeling to start the fire with a kindling stick from the stove.

"I was a doctor, remember? I think I know where the heart is. I'll be needing the smaller needles. These won't do." She turned back to Caltha, who lay motionless, face pale. "You're lucky it wasn't something bigger, Cal."

"Yeah, lucky..." Caltha trailed off, the whites of her eyes peeked out under her half-closed eyelids, making her irises disappear.

"Needles, Raf!"

"There! Next to you!" Rafaella gestured to the spot near Lina's elbow. "I put them there, beside you on your left, in with the other ones." Rafaella moved to Lina's side. "I'll hold, you sew."

"Soak your hands first."

Rafaella showed her hands, still dripping with the clove mixture. "Come on, let's go!"

Rafaella held the wound steady as Lina stitched, threading the needle on one side, then the other. She held her finger at the base of the thread, looking up to meet Rafaella's eyes. "Okay. Now."

Rafaella poured the clove mixture along the edges of the wound. At the same moment, Lina pulled the thread taut, finishing off the knot at the end.

Caltha hadn't moved, the white slivers still pecking out from her eyelids.

"She's lost a lot of blood," Lina said. "We should let her rest, check on the others."

"I'm not moving. The others are fine, few cuts and bruises. Nothing to worry about."

"Raf, you should leave her and..."

"I said I'm not moving! I'll be here when she wakes up. You check if you want to. Go! Get out of here!"

Lina left the cabin, muttering under her breath.

Rafaella sat in a chair by Caltha's side, elbows resting on her knees. Rafaella wiped a stray tear with her elbow, the droplet soaking into the fabric. She blew out a breath. Caltha's face was pale, beads of sweat glistening in the firelight. "Come on, Cal, stay with me." She lifted a hand to Caltha's face, smoothing the hair out of her eyes.

# 28

201 closed her eyes, listening to the straw rustle beneath her head. Reno shifted his position at the other side of the cabin. She knew that sleep was inevitable. Though she tried to resist the pull, she felt herself slipping once more.

201 dreamed of a field. The field was filled with crops, swaying in the breeze. She looked down at herself, an oversized tunic covering her front. She pulled at the fabric, staring down at her tiny fingers as they fumbled with the material.

*I am a little one.*

Gerd? Gett, no Gerda. My name is...

*Gerda.*

201 ran alongside a stream, humming a tune, the sound foreign and senseless to her ears. She followed the stream, watching a leaf, no, her leaf, she corrected herself, as it made its way along rocks, cascading through the channels, following the water as it rushed past her feet. She held her stick, poking the leaf every now and then to push it out when it became stuck in bundles of twigs gathered at the water's edge. The leaf dislodged from the twigs, drifting on the rushing water, pulling away from her reach.

Dust drifted up from the ground, sparkling in the light before everything became black.

Hoofbeats. The ground shook, jarring 201 and echoing the beat of her heart. The hoofbeats grew stronger as figures on horseback appeared from the blackness, illuminated by a dull blue light that flickered, making her eyes twitch. The lights buzzed, a steady drone filling her senses. The field narrowed, walls of stone solidifying around her as the daylight faded.

The hoofbeats faded as the figures surrounded her. She looked up at the robed silhouettes, craning her neck to try to get a glimpse of their faces.

"Hello, little one," said a voice.

*I know you. I know you.*

"How pleasant to see you again, Gerda. Or should I call you 201?" His face was shrouded in a hooded robe, glimpses of his features poking out from the darkness within.

201 began to sweat, drips of perspiration making their way from the back of her neck, trailing down over the gentle bumps of her spine.

"I know you," she said.

The figure laughed. The sound prickled at 201's shoulder, a tingle spreading across her back.

*I know you.*

"Show yourselves. I am not afraid." 201 took a shaky breath, clenching her tiny fists by her sides.

"Yes, little one. We will do as you say, since you asked so nicely." The voice chilled her blood but she refused to cry out, her feet remaining in place.

"But you are wrong about being afraid. You will be afraid. Fear is what makes us real."

The hooded figure raised his hands, lifting the robe from his head. Before the hood could fall to the ground, 201 knew who it was that had spoken.

*Do not run.*

201 squeezed her eyes shut, willing the figures to disappear. She opened them once more to find the features of Officer Jorg smiling down at her, the face that she had tried so hard to block from her memories, memories that refused to stay hidden.

"I have missed you, 201." 201 felt her stomach turn, bile rising in her throat.

The other figures removed their robes to reveal Officers Morton and Ryan. They opened their mouths to speak, the sound amplifying as the voices joined together in unison.

"We have missed you, 201," the voices said. "Come back to us..."

"No!" 201 tried to cover her ears but the voices became stronger, echoing in her ears from within. The three voices joined once more, the sound becoming shrill, jarring her senses.

"Internee Beth 259201. We shall now send our gratitude to Pinnacle Officer Cerberus and FERTS, for our daily provision and protection from those who would seek to strike against our Vassals, our Fighters and our Internees."

"No!"

201 awoke to the sound of her own breathing, the sun streaming across her face. She shivered, though

the beam of light was warm. It reminded her of the sliver of light from her quarters at Epsilon, at Beta, at Omega.

*At FERTS.*

201 watched the sleeping form of Reno, his breaths almost too soft for her to hear. 201 wondered for a moment if he was breathing at all. His chest began to move, rising a little, then falling again.

201 huddled in the corner of the cabin, nestled in the warm straw that prickled at her back and legs. She could still see the figures from her dream, the hoods falling from their faces, their voices united, joined as one as they spoke those words, the words that made no sense yet made perfect sense after all...

*Fear is what makes us real.*

The words swirled in her mind, filtering through her consciousness, weaving their way through pathways she did not know and was yet to understand. The words seemed so simple, yet they could not mean what she suspected, surely that was impossible. 201 shook the images from her head, attempting to focus on something, anything other than the faces of Officer Jorg, Morton and Ryan. The three of them, joined together, again the thread wove through her mind and again she grappled with the complexity of the notion.

The image, the *symbol*, rose up again, the long, winding line, curving from the middle, expanding ever outwards. She held the symbol in her mind, memorizing the shape, the simplicity and beauty of its design. It spoke to her, not through words, but through a feeling. From the inside to the outside, that is where the line forged its path.

*From the inside to the outside.*

It was hers now, this strange symbol carved into rock so long ago. It was waiting, she felt, waiting for someone to see and understand. She did not profess to understand it to any great degree, but a sense of the image was growing, slowly taking shape within her being. Within her essence. But the symbol moved both ways, she realized. The path was ever changing, moving, reimagined and fluid as the water of the stream.

*From the outside to the inside.*

She attempted to hold the image behind her eyes, following the line from the outside to the inside, going deeper within her mind, past the sound of Wilcox screaming, past the thoughts and noise to the place where she was quiet, where she was still. The place where she was aware, senses deprived, seeing less but somehow seeing *more.*

It was of no use. The words were louder this time, too loud. They reverberated through her mind once more and she was unable to stop the voices as they joined in adulation to give thanks to the Pinnacle Officer and FERTS. The words repeated, drowning out her thoughts.

She began to sweat, hunched over in the corner, birds singing outside the window, the sun shining down, a scent of wildflowers in the air. She clutched her stomach as the words mocked her, repeating as she drifted back to a fitful sleep.

*Fear is what makes us real.*
*Fear is what makes us real.*
*Fear.*

# 29

201 awoke to the sound of the cabin door crashing open. Rafaella stood in the doorway, looking between Reno and 201.

"You their leader?" she asked Reno.

Reno looked up. "Yes, I..."

He was silenced by Rafaella's fist connecting with his cheekbone. He lurched to the right, sliding down the wooden wall. Reno groaned, spitting blood into the straw.

"That's for Cal. You're lucky I don't..." she trailed off, looking at 201. "What's with you?"

"What?"

"Your uniform." She gestured at the stain.

201 looked down, unaware for a moment of how she must look with her jumpsuit covered in blood and her face bruised and swollen.

"Raf... Rafaella. I need to speak with you." 201 widened her eyes, trying to convey the importance of her statement. Her eyes refused to cooperate, one of them still swollen from the encounter with 299. "I need to speak with you, alone."

"I don't think so. Who'd you kill? It wasn't one of ours, so who was it?"

"201?" Reno edged himself up the wall, flexing his jaw. "What is she saying? You told me…"

"Don't make me say it, Raf." 201 squeezed her eyes shut, attempting to block out Reno's furious stare.

"Only my friends call me Raf." Rafaella leaned down, her eyes wild. "Who did you kill?"

"I can't…" 201 edged back towards the corner of the cabin.

"Who did you kill?" Rafaella shouted, banging her fist on the floor, the sound muffled by the straw. 201 felt the jolt go through her, sweat breaking out along her arms.

She took a deep breath, looking over Rafaella's shoulder to meet Reno's eyes. "I expired Pinnacle Officer Wilcox."

Reno sucked in a breath. 201 looked past Rafaella to see Reno staring at her, his olive skin becoming pale.

Rafaella knelt one knee on the straw. "I don't believe you. Even we weren't crazy enough to try something like that."

"Check my boot." Rafaella looked at her, one eyebrow raised. "No, the other one. You will find it there."

Rafaella felt around 201's ankle, fingers closing around cold metal. She pulled it out, turning it over in her palm. The regulation nail file was sharpened to a deadly point, smeared with the dried blood of Pinnacle Officer Wilcox.

"The wound..." whispered Reno from behind Rafaella. "That's the right size, the right shape. I didn't think of something like that. It's not even a weapon."

201 looked down at the straw, shaking her head. "No, it was not a weapon. But given enough thought, sharpened by time and patience, it was possible," said 201. "I tried to keep this from you, Reno, since you would have been forced to send me to Zeta Circuit, or perhaps expire me yourself, I suppose there is no difference now." She caught a glimpse of Reno, his eyes never leaving her face.

"Yes, Reno, I expired the Pinnacle Officer. I substituted myself for the Vassal, the 18Y Vassal that Pinnacle Officer Wilcox had chosen for the night. I stole a radio from the guards and I waited. I knew that Rafaella and the others would blow the beacon. All I had to do was make sure I was in the elevator when it happened. With the Pinnacle Officer, of course. He did not expect what happened next. He did not know I was the wrong Vassal until the elevator had stopped, but by then it was too late."

Reno studied her face, his eyes flat, before tearing his gaze away. When he met her eyes again he appeared to stare through her, through the wall of the cabin, as if fixed on an unknown place far in the distance.

*Now he knows,* said the voice of Pinnacle Officer Wilcox. *He will expire you before this night is over.*

201 laughed to herself, her senses tingling, a chill shooting through her. She felt her mind wavering,

ready to split from her body but she clenched her fists, determined to stay firmly in place. She cleared her throat, trying to keep the tremor from her voice. "Someone told me to use my mind rather than just my body. That is the reason, the only reason that I am here with you today. Your words taught me this, Reno. I have never forgotten them."

"This is my fault..." Reno shook his head.

"No, I did this. This was something I planned, alone. You could not have known," said 201, willing him to connect with something, any part of this that could make sense for him. The look on his face indicated that he would not be sharing her understanding of the situation.

"I hate to interrupt, but how did you know that we were going to blow the beacon?" asked Rafaella. "We didn't tell anyone so how did you know? Did someone tell you? Who was it?"

"No, nobody told me."

"You saw them," said Reno, understanding dawning on his face. "You saw all of them."

"What? How..."

"He's right. I could see you, in my mind. That's why I call you Raf."

"I think it's time for you to do some more talking." She bent down over 201, lifting her from the ground and slicing the ropes from her feet. "You're coming with me."

Rafaella turned to address Reno. "I'll be back with some food and blankets for you. Knock on the wall if you need anything, Petra and Kap are right outside."

She turned back to Reno when they reached the door. "Oh, and don't think about trying anything, Kap can be a little... unpredictable."

201 looked back to see Reno glaring at her through the door as it slammed shut.

# 30

The door to the cabin swung open, revealing Lina kneeling by the hearth, stoking the coals to rekindle the fire. Lina looked up, her white hair illuminated by the flames. 201 stopped in the doorway, eyes trained on Lina.

"Hello," said Lina.

Lina's hair was wild, mostly white with flecks of dark brown peeking through in streaks. Her olive skin was dark, much like the faces of the Internees of Kappa, those faces from her dreams, the Kappa Internees who chopped wood in the heat of the day, sweating and straining without complaint. Her eyes were a vibrant green, with a kind crinkle at the corner and a welcoming smile. Her neck was lined, little collections of grooves running together and fanning over her collarbone. She wore a white tunic paired with a blue cloth belt, dark leather pants and dark brown leather boots.

"You... you are over limit." 201 spoke softly, the words barely breathed.

Lina smiled. "Over limit?"

"I don't mean... what I mean is..." 201 struggled for the right words. "I have never seen anyone, one like us, who is over limit. Not like this." She stepped forward, reaching out and touching Lina's hair. It was soft and light under her fingers. 201's eyes followed the crinkles at her eyes, the little furrows above her eyebrows. 201 giggled to herself, touching Lina's cheek. Lina grinned at her, nodding, a slight look of confusion creeping in.

"201, this is Lina. Lina, 201." Rafaella closed the door, clapping Jotha on the back. He remained in place, saber drawn, guarding the door. Rafaella nudged 201 towards a seat by the fire.

201 turned back to Lina. "You made it. You made it past the limit. I am glad," 201 said. "I mean, I am glad that you are. I hope to be like you some day."

"Well... thanks then." Lina clapped 201 on the shoulder, thankfully her good one. "Come, you need something to eat, you look starved." Lina disappeared into the kitchen.

Rafaella turned from the doorway, raising an eyebrow. "What was that all about?"

"We do not make it to over limit in FERTS. The others... they do not understand what this means. If you were an Internee, you would be expired by now. I am 24Y," said 201, gesturing to her insignia, the red numbers glowing in the gentle light of the cabin. "26Y is over limit. I did not have long to go before I was expired as well."

"Tell me about Zeta Circuit. Many of the Internees were taken there, but they do not understand what it was, aside from the fact that they knew they were to be... expired as you call it, at some point."

"That is the idea," said 201, leaning back against the chair. The coverings were soft, warmed from the heat of the fireplace. 201 felt the need to rest once more, but decided on shifting to keep her back straight in order to remain alert. "None of the Officers know of Zeta Circuit except the ones who are stationed there. Even Reno, he does not know. The Pinnacle Officer keeps one Circuit from the other, hiding each set of processes so nobody knows what happens there except for the Pinnacle Officer, and his second-in-command, Officer Cerberus. Cerberus, who is now the Pinnacle Officer of FERTS."

"They have a new Pinnacle Officer now?"

"Yes. The Pinnacle Officer is gone and another has risen in his place. There will be no end to this."

"And you know all this? How?"

"Yes, I know... I know some things. I dreamed of these things, saw them as I lay awake or when I slept. The images come to me..." She scratched her forehead, flicking off a dried flake of blood. "I do not always understand their meaning, but I see things that I now know to be true."

"Like us," said Rafaella.

"Yes, like you, Cal, Adira, Petra, Jotha and the others. I had not seen Lina though. She was not there when I watched you go through the plan."

"I still don't understand. You say you saw us. How could you have known..."

"20:15 regroup at Zeta, blow doors. 20:20 lead Zeta Circuit out the door. 20:25 sneak out, get through suspension zone. 20:30 regroup and arm up. Does any of this seem familiar?"

"Yes but..."

"Except you were wrong about the time you would blow the beacon. Something went wrong, I had to readjust my own plan."

"The charge didn't go off." Rafaella nodded, leaning forward in her chair and resting her elbows on her knees. "There was something up with the wiring, had to check it."

"I didn't see that. Like I said, I don't see everything, sometimes it makes no sense, but this time I knew something would go wrong, the timings were out..."

"So you still risked it? Knowing that the timings were wrong?"

201 nodded. "It was worth it."

"How?"

"At worst, I would have provided a distraction in order for you to get away. Zeta Circuit would be safe."

"No, at worst, we would have been killed, all of us. So many things could have gone wrong. Surely you know that?"

"I did not allow myself to think of that possibility. I had to focus. I did not expect to be here, I thought I would be expired before the end of that night."

"And Zeta would be safe."

"But that was not my only plan."

"No, you expired Pinnacle Officer Wilcox, an outrageous risk, if you ask me. If I was to take a guess,

I would say that you lost your mind, maybe a long time ago."

"That may be true," said 201. "It did not seem to be impossible to me. All I could see was the plan, and then..."

"Your escape."

"Yes."

Lina came through the doorway, handing bowls of soup to Rafaella and 201.

"What is this?"

"What do you mean?" asked Lina. "The soup? You have never had it before?" 201 shook her head. "It's just spicebush, carrot, onion, potatoes and beans. Trust me, you'll like it." She reached out her hand to stop 201, spoon poised at her mouth. "Just wait for it to cool down first, you'll burn your mouth."

201 put down her spoon, looking at the soup as the ingredients swirled in her bowl. She had never seen food like this, food that wasn't in the square shape of regulation protein, the watery, nothing taste that she had grown to endure. Lina left to make a pot of tea, humming as she made her way around the kitchen.

"So how is it you come to be with the Epsilon Fighters then?" Rafaella's face grew hard. "How is it you come to be here, attacking our camp?"

201 lifted the spoon to her nose, the aroma of the soup weaving its way around her. The fragrance was like nothing she had experienced before, warming her senses and making her feel a sense of something...

something familiar yet unrecognizable. She placed the spoon back in the bowl. It was still too hot.

"I was captured. Recaptured, I suppose you could say, though Reno did not see it that way. He saw it as a rescue from the mercenaries. These rogues that I have never seen." She looked up at Rafaella. "I was so close, Raf," she whispered. "I nearly made it."

"Yeah, well you're not out yet. You attacked our camp. I'm not going to let you out to wander around where you could attack any of us."

"I wouldn't do that."

"Yeah, you say that. You tell your leader, this Reno, that you killed a mercenary. You arrive here to attack the camp with the Epsilon Fighters. You tell me you killed Pinnacle Officer Wilcox. Forgive me if I don't believe every word you say."

"Last night. That ember you saw last night. That was me as well. It was a warning."

"Yeah, well you say a lot of things, and now Cal's injured, badly. I don't take well to attacks, friendly or otherwise."

201 thought it wise to remain silent if she was to get a chance to taste the soup. Just inhaling the aroma had been intoxicating so far. She had once before ventured to try the strange roots growing by the river, and though they did not agree with her, they were preferable to regulation protein. The regulation protein was familiar, predictable. She was used to the taste, though she did not care for it. It was always as expected, never varying to any great degree. This 'soup' as it was called, was a wild, chaotic mixture of

items she neither recognized nor understood. The mixture of fragrances alone was overwhelming.

201 raised the spoon to her lips, sipping slowly. The taste exploded across her tongue, strange, earthy, warm, the taste of comfort, memories of something she could not understand, yet felt she knew somehow, yet could not possibly know. One word trailed through her mind as she sipped at the spoon, allowing the flavor to wash over her, filling her senses with warmth and comfort.

*Home.*

# 31

Everything was dark. 201 reached out to touch something, anything but she was floating, swimming in darkness. But she was not alone.

"Help me," said a voice.

201 reached out again, stretching her fingers to make contact.

"I can't find it. It's too dark. Help me."

201 spun her awareness to find the source of the voice.

Caltha was floating, spinning, curled in on herself. She looked so young and scared. Her eyes sprang open to stare at 201.

"Cal?"

201 gasped, opening her eyes to find she had slipped out of consciousness in front of the fire. The voices of Lina and Rafaella stopped as they both turned to face her.

"What did you just say?" asked Rafaella.

201 blinked at her.

"You said 'Cal', I heard you." She looked over at Lina. "We both heard you." Rafaella leaned closer to 201. "You don't get to call her that. Why did you say her name?"

"I saw her," 201 whispered.

"I don't believe you. You had a dream, that's all."

"I saw her, Raf. She's trapped. She can't get out. Can't find a way out. She was scared..."

"Shut up!" Rafaella stood up, eyes glistening. "Get her out of here! I don't want to see her face. Get her out!"

Jotha strode towards 201, grasping her wrists behind her back, securing them with rope. He pushed her towards the door. 201 struggled in his grasp, turning back to Rafaella.

"You have to talk to her, Raf. She needs you."

Rafaella refused to look at 201, turning back to the fire.

Jotha pushed 201 along the path towards the back cabins. 201 saw strange animals in fields, the sound of voices filtering out from the cabins, the glow of warmth seeping out through the windows.

"I was telling the truth, Jotha."

Jotha gripped her wrist. "How do you know our names?"

"I told Raf already. I saw you, dreamed of you, long before I arrived here."

"Well, that's just great."

"You heard what I said in there. Last night... that ember you saw, that was me. I was telling the truth. You have to talk to Raf, make her understand. Cal's in trouble. She can't get out. She's afraid. You have to do something!"

"I'll keep that in mind," said Jotha. He led 201 towards the door, flanked by Petra and Kap.

"He's pretty mad," said Kap, gesturing over his shoulder to Reno inside the cabin. "Been yelling for a while now but he's quieted down a bit."

Jotha nodded, allowing them to open the door. He pushed 201 inside.

"Make sure they don't kill each other," said Jotha. "You hear anything worse than yelling, call for me."

Kap nodded, placing a hand on Jotha's shoulder. Petra gave him a grin, resting the crossbow on her lap.

"You ever going to sleep?" asked Kap.

"Yeah, just not yet." Jotha gave him a smile.

# 32

201 lay face down in the straw, twisting her body in order to flip over into a sitting position. She edged back to where she thought she would find the wall. There was barely any moonlight to make out shapes in the darkness.

"Traitor." Reno's voice seemed to come from beside her. Too close. He growled, launching himself at 201 and butting his head against her midsection. She rolled, edging along the wall, straw shuffling at her feet, making too much noise for him not to hear.

She heard Reno rustle in the straw, ready to pounce again. This time 201 was ready for him. She waited until she heard the crunch of straw beneath his feet and threw herself down the wall, hitting the straw beneath. The satisfying thud of Reno's head against the wall reverberated through the cabin. He slid down the wall, panting.

"Stop it. You will hurt yourself," she said.

She heard another thud as he banged his head against the wall, breathing out in a rush. "I trusted you, 201," he said.

"So you trusted me. I trusted Harold too. I trusted him to stop Officer Ryan from hurting me. He did not help me. I trusted you. You would have been forced to expire me at some point. I suppose you trusted Wilcox as well. Your trust in FERTS will be your downfall."

"You lie," he said.

"No, you will find that I speak the truth," said 201, shuffling back to rest against the wall. "Or perhaps you will not. I really do not know."

"I thought you saw everything. How can you not know?"

"I do not see everything, as you put it. I see things, some of them make sense, others do not. Sometimes I wish that I did not know about FERTS in the way that I do now."

"You dare to speak of FERTS in this way. I should..."

"You should what? Expire me? Knowing what I know, it is the same as being expired. You complain of these ropes, this cabin. This is nothing! I sleep on straw tonight, and yes, I am bound. But that is nothing compared to what the Internees must endure. Perhaps you will think of Beta and Omega Circuit as you sleep, knowing that their nights may end with an Officer in their doorway, ordering them to strip."

Reno exhaled, banging his head on the wall once more.

"Or perhaps you will think of Epsilon Circuit. The ones who are sold to Vendees for their private entertainment. They fight, then they are taken. Then they are expired."

"What?"

"You didn't know," she muttered to herself. "Of course you didn't know. You are the trainer. You know what the trainer must know, nothing more. Now I understand," she said.

"How dare you..."

"Or perhaps you will think of Kappa, the Internees with their aching backs, the strain from chopping wood is too much you see. But they know that if they flinch, it they complain, as you complain of these ropes," she added, shuffling her feet. "They know they will be sent to Zeta Circuit. It makes no difference. When they fall, they are sent just the same. And Zeta Circuit will burn, always burning, waiting again to be filled."

"What about Alpha Field?"

201 sighed. "Did you know, Reno, what the plan would be if your attack on the camp failed?"

"What do you mean?"

"Pinnacle Officer Cerberus had a plan, did he not. Would it be so strange to think that he may have had a backup plan?"

"Well, the Pinnacle Officer would always have a plan. It is his duty to protect the Vassals from mercenaries. That is the main duty of the Pinnacle..."

"Mercenaries? Mercenaries? FERTS is built on a lie, Reno. And that lie is this: There are no mercenaries."

"But..."

"No, you do not understand! There *is* no threat from mercenaries!"

"No, this time I know you are wrong, 201. I have seen them, once. They wore cloaks. I know of others who have seen them. FERTS was built to protect..."

"All mercenaries are Officers of FERTS! They are acting under Pinnacle Officer Cerberus' command, and Wilcox before him. They wear the clothing of mercenaries and take the horses, but they are Officers in disguise. This, *this*, has been the truth all along."

"No," Reno's voice was small. "No, this cannot be..."

"These attacks were designed to create fear. That is what I have learned. I dreamed of this, Reno. They told me, though I did not understand at the time. The words they spoke to me, they make perfect sense now. Fear is what makes us real."

"You are senseless, 201. Stop this."

"Yes!" 201 laughed to herself, her voice trailing off. "Perhaps you are right. But how can one see what I see and remain as before? It is not possible. But what I say is true. The rogues are nothing but a vision, a creation of FERTS itself. A story to scare the Vassals at night, a story of a sworn enemy to keep the Epsilon Fighters dreaming of their most important battle, when all along, they were fighting nothing but a shadow. These rogues, these mercenaries, Reno, are nothing but dust, they are mist, a reflection on the water that ripples and distorts when the wind blows. They are no more real than the idea that you can catch the wind in your hand and hold it forever. You will never catch them. You will never find them because they move among you, you fool, FERTS is the enemy!"

"You have... you have truly lost your senses 201."

201 chuckled to herself. "Yes, perhaps I have lost my senses after all."

"But I know... they attacked the townships..."

"The attack was a lie, Reno."

"I knew of townspeople who were slaughtered. It was no lie. You are mistaken, 201."

"No! The people were slaughtered, yes that is true, but the lie is that the rogues were responsible. What better way to keep the townspeople in line than to bring to them a threat that they cannot defeat? How clever of Pinnacle Officer Wilcox, how clever to pay the Officers, those who are known to him, to do the deal with rations and the promise of a few Vassals. To think it could create a thing such as this."

"But FERTS was created to protect the Internees, keep them safe and hidden from the townships in order to ensure the security of..."

"Senseless fool!" shouted 201. "FERTS was built on a lie. A lie that you helped create, whether you were aware of it or not."

"I didn't know, 201," he said. "I would not... it is not right, what has been done."

"You thought it was right with protection as your excuse! Now you think it is not right? I do not believe you. You only believe the reason is wrong, not the methods. THAT is the problem!"

"No, I didn't know about Zeta Circuit, about what you may know about Alpha..." he choked on his words.

"But you knew 232 would be expired! You watched her, watched her as she said those words and you did nothing."

"No! I had to choose a Fighter. I knew, yes, I suspected, maybe I knew that whoever was to fight 299 would not be victorious. But Games Operator Farrenlowe already had someone in mind. Who? You. I had to give him another, you were not ready... I didn't want..."

"What about what I want, Reno? I want my companion back! You took 232 from me! The only companion I have ever known and all for the entertainment of your precious Officers. Or should I say *rogues*."

Reno made a wounded noise, the sound coming from deep within his chest. "This is the worst day of my life," he said.

"Of your life? Of your life? You did not endure Officer Jorg when you were 12Y. You did not spend every night since then afraid to sleep for fear of what you might see. You were not taken and beaten by Officer Morton and Ryan. You did not watch your companion..." She banged her boots on the floor. "She was important, Reno! We are all important! And you took her from me!" 201 laughed, a chesty, breathy sound. She stared into the blackness, seeing nothing.

"201..."

"But that, that was not the worst day. Not even then. The worst day was after I escaped, I felt what freedom was like, if only for a brief time. I watched the sun rise without regulations and I was real, I was something more than what I am now. The worst day was when you found me... with the fighting creature." 201 laughed again. "After all I have seen, that was the worst, and it makes no sense, yet it makes perfect sense. Now I have known freedom I know what I do not have. That, that, is worse."

# 33

Petra looked up at Kap as the raised voices from the cabin reached their position.

"What do you think they are shouting about?" she asked, tucking her bright red hair behind her ear. She looked over at Kap, her blue eyes muted by the dimness of the light. Kap grinned down at her, scratching his dark red beard, a number of recently sprouted white hairs lining either side of his chin.

"I don't know. I don't get it," Kap said. "That's an Officer and an Internee in there. Every Internee I have met from Zeta Circuit, even after all they have faced in this time, they still feel it."

"What?"

"The guilt. They still feel it, even though they know they did nothing wrong, they believe that maybe there was something they could have done differently. Maybe thought they could make things right somehow. It makes no sense, knowing what they know, but that's what they think."

"Why do they think like that anyway?" asked Petra. She glanced around the camp, watching smoke drifting from the chimneys of the other cabins. "If that was me, I would have said no, I would have fought. Why don't any of them do this? I don't get it."

She shook her head, playing with a spare bolt, flipping it over in her fingers. "I would have run, I would have done anything to get out of there, so why? Why do they just accept..."

"I don't think it's that easy," said Kap. Petra shot him a look. "Well, the way I see it, I may be wrong of course, I mean, what do I know? But they were raised in FERTS from birth. This is all they know. They have spent every moment trying to fulfil an ideal, to be something that seems so foreign to you and me. But this is all they know. Their training..."

Petra nodded, running a hand through her hair. "Yeah. You're right, you're right. I wasn't thinking..."

"It's just they way they've always been. It's their training..."

"No, not their training, Kap," said Petra. "Their *programming*. They have been conditioned to think the way they do. I wasn't thinking straight. They're conditioned, that's what it is. I suppose it's true of many of the Officers as well."

"Conditioned?" he scratched his beard, leaning against the door of the cabin as the voices began shouting again. "You mean brainwashed."

"I haven't heard of that word before."

"It means the same thing. Conditioned, as you call it. The lies they're told in there. It's all they know. They go against that, they not only go against the Officers but their friends in there as well. They really don't have a choice, in the end."

"This is no simple thing, is it?"

The shouting started up again, their muffled voices seeping through the cracks in the door.

"No. It's not."

"So what about them?" She gestured to the door behind her. "What's their story?"

"That's the part I don't get. They keep yelling at each other, but no Internee I have seen would ever dare yell at an Officer, especially not a higher ranking one, like that one in there. So why? Why this one?" said Kap, his forehead scrunching up in concern.

"This one," said Petra, turning to the door and listening to the raised voices. "She's different to the others somehow."

"Yeah," Kap said, chuckling to himself. "She's different all right. Seems like she's not right in the mind, hate to say it. Her eyes just don't look right." He shook his head. "I don't know, I'm rambling on. It might have just been the light, I don't know." He flipped the saber over in his hand, scratching a mark off the blade. "I just... I knew an old soldier once, Torrel, this was after the war, long time ago, too long for you to remember anyway. I brought him a few things from time to time. He used to just sit there, staring through me. When I talked to him, he looked through me even when he was looking right at me. Like he was seeing something else, something that I couldn't see. Guess he just saw one too many things and something broke in there." He tapped his temple. "Never could get it back." Kap sat down on the chair by the front door, resting his saber on his knee. "That one in there..." He cocked his thumb to the door between them. "Well, she's got that look in her eyes too."

# 34

"So what's the plan now?" asked Reno. His voice drifted across the darkness of the cabin to reach 201. He sounded far away, yet the way the sound carried made him seem closer somehow. She lay with her eyes open, seeing nothing, but staring up at the ceiling just the same.

"You think I'd tell you, that is, if I had one?" She smiled in the dark.

"You mean you didn't have a plan, after all this?"

"I had a plan, but you and the fighting creature destroyed it. Now I can do nothing but take what little choice I have been given. No, this is not freedom for me, but compared to FERTS, it is better. And now you must endure, just as I do. Still, I care for you, Reno, even if you are a fool."

Reno let out a nervous laugh, the straw rustling beneath him.

"That's the first time I have heard you laugh, Reno."

"Hm," he muttered. "But surely you have thought about this, what you will do. Perhaps you dreamed something?"

"I cannot will a dream into existence, Reno. They come when they come, I see only what I am allowed to see."

"What does that mean?"

"Sometimes... well, it doesn't matter now if I tell you. When I expired Pinnacle Officer Wilcox he became bound to me. I do not profess to understand how it works. Perhaps those who expire others are not aware of this when it happens. But I am aware, and it frightens me."

"You mean Wilcox, he's..."

"In my head, yes. He speaks to me, tries to confuse me, blocks me from seeing what it is I need to see."

"But how?"

"I don't know. But understand this. I carry the weight of expiring the Pinnacle Officer within me. It is always there, in one form or another. But Wilcox..." She lowered her voice to a whisper, turning her head in the straw. "The number bound to him is beyond my comprehension. There are so many, Reno. So many. I hear them crying in my dreams and I can do nothing to help them. The first... Beth, the one he knew before he began his plan. It is her voice I hear the loudest."

"But can't you do something? Can't you stop them?"

"I can shut them out... sometimes. Sometimes they are too loud." She adjusted her head in the straw, fatigue creeping in.

"What will you do?"

"What I do doesn't matter. Not at this moment, anyway. What matters is what Pinnacle Officer Cerberus will do."

"You're talking about the plan, the backup plan you mentioned."

"Did you ever wonder what his plan would be if your attack failed? What are your thoughts on this?"

"I... I suppose I did not consider the possibility that we could fail."

"After all you have taught me?" 201 rubbed her wrists together to relieve the itch of the ropes. "Well it seems that Pinnacle Officer Cerberus did consider this possibility. His plan was simple. If you fail in your attack, he destroys it."

"What?" Reno sucked in a breath.

"You know now they have a backup plan, and you are a part of that plan, but fear not, Reno, you will not see it coming. They will burn this camp, with you in it!"

"He wouldn't. I have known Cerberus for a long time, you are mistaken again, it would seem."

"He would, and he will. This is not for protection, for your rescue, this is to tie off any loose threads. You, Reno. You are the loose thread, as am I. For now we are both rogues, it would seem." She chuckled. "You are a rogue for following orders. I am a rogue for disobeying regulation. It is strange, is it not?"

"So we are the only rogues, it would seem."

"Yes. The only ones."

# 35

Caltha lay on a bed by the fire, her skin pale and covered with sweat. Rafaella felt her neck, finding a pulse so faint that she had to close her eyes to feel the feeble rhythm.

"Come back to me, Cal," she whispered.

Caltha did not move. Her eyes were still beneath her eyelids. Rafaella checked her breathing, holding her hand above Caltha's mouth. Satisfied, she sat back in her chair, wiping her sweating palms on her tunic.

"Come on, Cal."

Caltha floated in darkness, hearing the faint voice in the distance. She could barely make out the sound. It sounded like Rafaella, but she could not make her way towards the voice, she could only float. She listened again.

Nothing, nothing, only darkness, feeling nothing.

Her mind flashed, pictures forming in front of her eyes, too quick to recognize or understand. They were faces, things that she had seen, perhaps things that she knew, it went by too quickly to make any sense.

One face became clear, the unruly black beard that always felt softer than it looked, the sweep of hair above his forehead, his skin, darkened by the sun, his dark eyes squinting at her. She remembered everything down to the veins in his neck, the way they stood out while he was chopping wood.

*Renn?*

He smiled that familiar smile. She remembered the way he used to watch her with an amused smile when he thought she wasn't looking. She remembered how he smelt of cut grass and wood shavings, and sometimes his hands smelt like the leather he wove and shaped into belts. She remembered the first time he gave her one of his woven bracelets, the way he acted as though it was nothing special.

*Renn? It can't be you. You're...*

*Dead?*

*Yes. Then I'm...*

*Don't worry Cal, I'll stay with you while you figure it out. You won't be alone in here, I promise. I'm sorry you have to go through this, I really am. I wish there was something I could do.*

*Don't make me remember, Renn. I don't want to remember. Renn?*

There was no answer.

The memories of that day came to Caltha's mind, much as they had in the past when she was conscious and able to push them aside. She could feel them coming, swarming throughout her being, filling her mind until she was there, living and breathing in those awful moments before everything changed, the day where her life ended and another, darker one began. This time she knew, once the memories started, they would not relent. This time there would be no escape.

The bone whistle pierced the silence of the evening, shrill and jarring. Symon had been keeping watch that night, a night that was uneventful, until now. Symon was shouting something but Caltha could not make out the words. Rafaella was up and heading for the weapons store before the second whistle had a chance to ring out.

Caltha looked at Renn. They locked eyes for a long moment, Caltha seeing something in his eyes that she had not seen before.

"Cal," he whispered. "Get Adira. Hide her in the closet. Try not to wake her. Keep her quiet somehow."

Caltha rushed to the bedroom, bundling Adira in her arms. Adira stirred, her little fists bunched in balls by her cheeks. Her eyes were heavy as she looked around at her surroundings. Caltha rocked her from side to side, humming a lullaby. If she could just get her to the closet she could arm herself and stand with the others. She tucked Adira in the bottom of the closet, swaddled in blankets. She closed the door, making sure the bottom of the door was letting in enough air. She scrambled for her bone dagger, tucking it in her boot. Rafaella would bring her spatha, she was sure of it, providing she and Renn could get back from the weapons store in time. The bone dagger would have to do for now. Her hand closed on the carved wooden handle as Symon's voice rang out through the camp, the words she hoped she would never hear reaching her ears.

"Incoming!" The whistle sounded, shorter this time, squeaking at the end. Caltha gripped her bone dagger tighter.

"Mercenaries! Incoming!" The whistle sounded again. Adira's cry rang out from the closet. The sound of hoofbeats filled the camp.

"Incoming!" Symon's voice was cut off, leaving only the sounds of cheers and cries as metal clashed against metal.

They had made it inside the camp.

Caltha opened the closet, grabbing Adira's doll. She placed it in Adira's hands, touching her cheek.

"Adira." She crouched down beside her. "I need you to be quiet for me." She stroked her forehead, listening to the sounds of hoofbeats approaching. "I'm going outside for a little while. I need you to keep quiet until I come back." She looked around the darkened hallway, hearing the hoofbeats closing in. "You probably don't understand a word I'm saying but please, Adira. Please. Keep quiet. I love you." She kissed her cheek and closed the closet door.

Caltha stepped outside to find Rafaella, Bonni, Renn and Jotha lined up outside the main cabin. She could not see Symon anywhere and the lookout tower appeared empty.

The leader sat on horseback, surveying the group assembled before the cabin. The other four gathered the weapons, tucking them into saddlebags. Caltha watched her own spatha join them in the haul.

"I want that one. The tall one," said one of the mercenaries, pointing at Rafaella. The leader nodded, gesturing for him to go ahead. The mercenary closed in on Rafaella, struggling with her while the others laughed.

"Do you need some help, Jorg?"

Jorg glared, holding a knife to Rafaella's throat. "I've got it under control."

Jorg hoisted Rafaella to the back of his horse, leaping up behind her.

"I'm going ahead."

"Can't wait, Jorg?"

Jorg didn't bother to answer. He kicked the horse, galloping towards the cliffs.

"Raf!" Caltha shouted. The mercenaries turned to look at her. The leader smiled, his eyes glinting. "And you will do nicely for me." He dismounted, moving towards Caltha.

"Not going to happen," Renn said.

"What was that?" He turned to stare at Renn. "You're going to stop me? I don't think so." He grabbed at Caltha's arm.

"No!" Renn yelled, leaping towards the leader. A piercing wail broke out from the main cabin as Adira began to cry.

"Adira..." Caltha turned her head.

A bolt flew beside her, hitting the leader on the shoulder. Renn grappled with him, tumbling them to the ground. Caltha grabbed her bone dagger from her boot, rushing for the leader only to be stopped by another mercenary. Two more descended on Renn as Bonni struggled to get the one closest to her. Adira's cry merged with another, deeper cry and Caltha froze, her bone dagger deep in the mercenary's side. Another bolt flew, hitting the mercenary on Bonni's side as she rushed to Renn, dispatching the two mercenaries piled above him. She pulled the leader across the dirt. He was dead, eyes staring up to the night sky. Adira continued to cry as the sound of hoofbeats returning filled the camp.

Rafaella rode, dangling half astride the horse, her leg covered in blood, a looped gash on her right arm. The other mercenary was nowhere to be seen. Rafaella dismounted, everything slowing down as Symon limped from the lookout watch, crossbow in one hand, the other clamped over his bleeding arm. Caltha clambered over the bodies of the mercenaries.

Renn was not moving.

Adira screamed from within the cabin once more, breaking the silence.

A stream of blood ran from Renn's side. When Caltha lifted the flap of his tunic, a pattern of slashes revealed themselves, too many for her to stop the flow. She ripped her own tunic, screaming to Bonni and Jotha for more cloth, water, anything to stop the bleeding. She pressed down, Renn's eyes looking into her own. He smiled. "Look after Adira. She looks up to you." He coughed, blood tainting his bottom lip. "I love you," he said, breathing out one last time.

*No no no no no.*

"Renn!" Caltha screamed.

Rafaella rushed to Caltha, grabbing hold of her. Caltha struggled, pushing her away until she lost her strength.

Rafaella held Caltha, her eyes streaming, face grim. Jotha stood with Bonni and Symon, hands clenching uselessly by his sides. Caltha hit the dirt with her hands, balling them up into fists as Adira wailed louder. Caltha's voice cracked as it rang out throughout the camp, the sound mingling with Adira's scream.

"Renn!"

# 36

201 awoke with a shout.

"Cal!" she yelled, kicking her feet against the straw.

"What, what is it?" Reno's voice made its way over to her corner of the cabin.

201 drew her legs up, curling in on herself. "Officer Jorg... Raf expired him, she expired him. Renn..."

"What are you talking about, 201?" Reno edged closer, his voice soft.

"Cal's trapped there. She has to watch, over and over again. She has to watch Renn..." 201 let out a breath, tears falling on her jumpsuit. "She thinks it's her fault..."

"Is there... is there something I can do?" Reno spoke the words as if he had never heard himself speak them before.

"There's nothing you can do." She raised her voice, kicking at the wall of the cabin. "Let me out of here! I need to speak to Raf! I need to speak to her now!"

"What the..." The door opened to reveal Kap, his large frame blocking the door, saber at his side.

"I need to speak to Raf!" 201 shouted.

"She doesn't want to speak to you, kid." Kap shook his head. "Sorry, but she told Jotha already. Nobody gets to talk to her, especially not you."

"This is important!" said 201.

Kap looked at 201, his face softening. "Look I understand. If it was up to me... but it's not. You don't get to talk to Raf. Not now, anyway." He smiled at her. "The thing about Raf is... she gets mad easily, but she'll come around. It just might take a bit of time for her to see things differently."

"We don't have time!"

"201..." said Reno.

"No, Reno, I can't let this go. She can't get out."

"Look, I can't help you, kid," said Kap, turning to leave.

"Wait..." said 201. "If I can't see Raf... you have to get a message to her. Tell her..." 201 thought for a moment, an image forming in her mind.

Images of reeds, swaying in the current of the river. Stars, so many stars, the reflection of moonlight on the surface of the river. She saw Raf and Cal, so small, Raf towering over Cal, helping her walk through difficult terrain. Raf and Cal alternating between sharing a satchel for a pillow and fighting over it in order to sleep under a mass of stars so beautiful that they did not look real. Raf tending to Cal's ankle, bringing her strawberries until half of Cal's face was stained red with the juice. Raf and Cal winding their way through forests, following the river, eating by their fire, laughing and chattering.

"Tell her... tell her to read the story... the one about Hett and Wenda. Tell her to read it to Cal."

"What? That story's for kids."

"Just tell her! Tell her to read the story to Cal! Please, you have to listen to me!"

"Okay, fine. I'll tell her. Can't guarantee that she'll listen to me though."

"Please..."

"I'll try, okay? That's all I can promise."

201 smiled at him, a single tear escaping. "Thank you." She leaned back against the wall, wiping her cheek. "Thank you, thank you."

Kap shook his head, closing the door behind him.

# 37

Rafaella sat in the chair by the fire. Caltha lay before her, hands by her sides. Rafaella had watched, waited for a sign of movement but in all this time, Caltha had not moved.

"Damn it, Cal," she whispered. "Why'd you have to go and change the plan?"

Caltha's face was smooth, devoid of expression. She looked so young, the usual laugh lines absent. It looked strange on her, unnatural.

Rafaella leaned back in her chair, a tear escaping from one eye. "This is my fault. I shouldn't have let you do this. I know it's what you wanted but I should have said no." She clenched her fist. "We always go together, that's how we've always done things."

Caltha's face appeared animated for a moment, the light of the flames dancing across her features. The way the shadows danced, her face appeared to move, curving into a smile, but Rafaella knew this was a trick of the light.

"Why'd you have to lead the second group, Cal? We're a team, we always work better as a team. That's the way it's always been. Why'd you have to do this?"

Lina appeared behind her, watching her from the doorway, arms folded.

"I let you do this and now look what happens. You were so busy trying to protect Adira that you forgot the most important thing. What would happen to Adira if something happened to *you*. You didn't think of that, did you?"

Rafaella leaned forward, elbows resting on her knees.

"Well now we know, and I can't do a damn thing to stop it. What's going to happen, Cal? She's already lost Renn, wasn't that enough? I mean... I know it's not your fault. None of this is your fault, it's mine. But I can't be what she needs, she needs you."

She stared into the fire, watching the flames rise and fall. The coals pebbled the bark of one of the logs, an orange glow running between the cracks.

"I should have been there to protect you, like always. I should have been there to watch you. I knew it was wrong. It was my responsibility and I let it happen. And now I might not get to tell you."

She ran a hand through her hair, sweeping the stray strands off her forehead, tucking them behind her ears. The strands were wet, a droplet falling in her ear. She rubbed it in annoyance.

"Damn it, Cal, I can't do this without you. It's you and me, that's how it is. You have to come back. Adira needs you. I need..." Rafaella turned her head, another tear falling. "It's done now. Can't take it back."

Rafaella blew out a breath. "I can't do this, Cal. This is not how it's meant to be. It's not the same if you're not there."

"Raf," Lina's voice came from the doorway. Rafaella wiped her eye, leaning back in the chair.

"Yeah, what is it?"

Rafaella looked up from her spot by the fire. Her back ached from leaning over Caltha. She wasn't sure how long she had been sitting in that spot. She supposed it must have been hours. She wasn't sure.

Lina stood in the doorway, leaning against the frame.

"It's been over a day, Raf. You need to sleep."

Rafaella rubbed a hand over her face. "I know, Lina. Sorry about before. I just can't... I can't just leave her here. I have to be here when she wakes up."

Lina walked over to the fire, crouching to warm her hands, knees clicking as she knelt. "You know that there's a possibility that..."

"I don't want to hear it. I can't do this. She's going to wake up, you'll see." Rafaella looked over to Caltha, willing her to move. Even her eyelids seemed frozen in place.

Lina sighed, rubbing her hands together. "Just make sure you get some sleep. You need to take care of yourself. You haven't moved from here, not even to eat."

"It can wait. Cal needs..."

"No, *you* need to eat something. You're no good to Cal or anyone like this."

"Fine, fine. I'll eat something." Rafaella stood, stretching her back. Lina led her to the kitchen, filling a bowl with vegetable stew. Rafaella looked down at it, prodding it with her spoon.

"Go on," said Lina. Rafaella tasted the stew, nodding as she refilled her spoon.

Kap knocked the back of his hand on the front door, coming through to join them in the kitchen.

"Kap." Rafaella glanced up at him, taking another bite. She paused when she saw the look on his face. "What is it? What's wrong?" asked Rafaella, standing up. Lina shot her a look. She sat back down and began eating again.

"I've got a message from the strange one."

Rafaella nodded, knowing exactly who he referred to.

"So? What is it?" Rafaella finished the stew, pushing the bowl away. Lina took the bowl, filling it again and pushing it back towards Rafaella.

"She wasn't making a whole lot of sense but she said it was important. She wanted you to read that book of Adira's to Cal. The one about Hett and Wenda." Rafaella paused, the spoon halfway to her lips.

"She knew about that?" she asked, taking another bite.

"Like I said, it doesn't make a whole lot of sense, but that's what she said."

"You're not joking, are you."

"No, you know I wouldn't joke about something like this. That's the message, she said it was important." He scratched at his beard. "Anyway I'm going to get Bonni and Vern to take over for us, we need to get some sleep."

"Yeah, thanks. Go, sleep, I'll see you tomorrow." She took another spoonful, chewing as she tapped her fingers on the wooden bench.

"What do you think that meant?" asked Lina.

"I don't know. Kap seemed serious though, and he's not usually like that."

"Are you going to do it?"

Rafaella looked up at her. "Right now, I'll try anything. I'll sing if I have to, and there aren't many of you who want to hear that."

Lina chuckled, patting Rafaella's shoulder. "You're right there. What can it hurt? Cal used to love those stories, you told me that yourself."

Later that evening, Rafaella sat by Caltha's side, a stack of string-bound papers in her lap. She opened to the first page. Looking down at the words, those words that had meant so much to her, to Cal, to Adira, made her stomach clench.

"I feel ridiculous, Cal. What am I doing?" She looked down at the papers again, the words blurring together, Lina's words fresh in her mind.

*What can it hurt?*

She wiped her eyes, taking another steadying breath.

"Long ago, in the township of Palomore, there lived two sisters..." She paused. This was the usual time that Caltha or Adira would say the next words, 'Hett and Wenda' but there were no sounds. It was strange, reading like this, watching Caltha's face, impassive and empty, like a mask.

"Damn it, Cal, can you even hear me?" She huffed out a breath, finding her place on the page.

"Hett was the eldest, and she protected Wenda wherever they went." She choked up when she read the next part. "Hett was keeping lookout this time, letting Wenda sleep." She took a shaky breath. "Wenda's ankle was healing nicely and soon she would be keeping pace with Hett once more as they made their journey along the banks of the river."

Caltha floated in blackness, her body curled in on itself, floating from nothing, towards nothing. She was so small, her body tiny and soft. She could hear sounds, sometimes they sounded like voices but she could not be sure. She tried to train her ears to listen out for the sounds. It was so lonely in here, warm but so dark. Another set of words came through, a little louder this time.

*Hett was keeping...*

Caltha listened for the sounds again.

*Wenda's ankle...*

The words were coming through clearer this time, forming a path in her mind. The words swirled before her, lighting a trail through the darkness, bringing trees into focus, the earth growing solid beneath her feet as her little body started to move, hearing the water rushing in her ears, she moved faster, her body growing bigger with each step. The river wound a path before her, laying the way forward as she stepped, jumping over logs and branches. She grew, her small hands growing larger by her sides as she pumped her fists, charging towards the voice, climbing, climbing up, ever higher until...

"They had seen no more bears..." said Rafaella, losing her place again. "Damn it, they had seen no more bears since their last encounter."

Rafaella's voice burst through her mind, the sound of rushing water roaring in her ears, the voice becoming louder and clearer.

Caltha sucked in a breath, her eyes struggling to open.

"And Hett would be happy if she never saw another bear again." Rafaella took another breath, turning the page. "Wenda could not even say the word..."

"Without glancing around to check the perimeter..." came the weak reply.

"Hey, who's telling this story, you or me?" asked Rafaella, chuckling to herself. "Wait... Cal?"

Caltha opened her eyes, squinting up at Rafaella.

"Cal!" Rafaella dropped the pages, tears falling to land on Caltha's tunic. "You're awake!" Rafaella grinned down at her. "You heard me. You heard the story. I didn't think it would work..."

"Yeah..." Caltha blinked, her eyes focusing on Rafaella's smile. "You dropped the story," she said.

"Sorry, sorry." Raf picked up the pages, resting them on a nearby table.

Cal blinked, lifting her head to glance around the room. "Where is everyone?"

"It's past midnight. I think most of them are asleep. Lina! Cal's awake!" Rafaella shouted. She let out a laugh, shouting out in celebration. Lina rushed into the room. She stopped when she saw Rafaella shouting, a huge smile on her face, beaming down at Caltha.

"You made it," she said, smiling down at her and patting her arm. "I'll go get you some tea."

Caltha lay her head back down. "Yeah, tea. Thanks, thanks Lina."

"You're really back." Rafaella laughed, squeezing her shoulder. "Don't go anywhere."

"That's funny." Caltha reached out, attempting to bat at Rafaella's arm but falling short.

Rafaella ran to the doorway, finding Jotha standing on the step. "What's going on? What's all the yelling about?"

"Cal's awake." Rafaella paced alongside the length of the long wooden bench at the entrance to the main cabin. "I was coming to wake you... I wasn't sure if I was going to bother anyone but..." She leaned against the wooden post, a tear slipping from her eye. "Just... just tell the whole camp, Cal's awake, she's okay," she whispered.

"Cal's awake?" Jotha's face brightened.

"Cal's awake!" Rafaella shouted out to the camp, stretching her arms out to the night sky. She let out a cry, laughing as she banged her fist against the post of the cabin. "Cal's awake!"

# 38

A cheer rose up from the camp, the muffled cries making their way through the window of the cabin.

"What *is* that?" asked Reno.

201 laughed, tears running down her cheeks. "She came back," she said, leaning back against the wall of the cabin. "She made it, Reno. Cal's okay."

"Cal?"

"The dark haired one. The one 299 wounded. She's okay. She woke up."

"Oh," said Reno. "Well, then, I'm glad."

The shouts rose up again, sounds of activity filtering through the camp. 201 wiped the corner of her eye with her sleeve. "That, that's what happens when someone cares, Reno. Don't you see? It worked. It really worked."

The door opened, Kap poking his head through the open door. "You hear that?"

"I hear it," said 201.

"I just came back to tell you, Cal made it." Kap turned to leave, hesitating with his hand on the door. He turned back to face 201. "You're okay, you know that?" Kap smiled at her, his features shadowed in the doorway. "You did good."

"I'm glad. I'm glad Cal's okay." 201 smiled at Kap as he backed away, closing the door.

A sound rose up from outside the doorway, a strange buzzing tone. 201 envisaged a carved wooden object, strange, twine-like lines running from one end to the other, vibrating under strong fingers as the lines were plucked, one by one. The sound filled 201's head, awakening a warm, pleasant feeling within her being.

"Is that..."

"It's music," said Reno.

"It doesn't sound like the piped music I used to hear in my chambers. What is this?"

"It's something I have not heard for a long time. This is real music, someone is playing that, right now."

"I like it," said 201, closing her eyes, allowing the sound to wash over her. It was like something she had known before, a reminder of a feeling she had never had, yet knew like it was her own.

"What you said before," said Reno, rustling in the straw as he shifted his position. "You mentioned a backup plan. What makes you so sure about that?"

"I thought I understood. I dreamed of a scroll, a set of orders. I thought I understood but I was wrong."

"What do you mean?"

"I thought they were your orders, but I was wrong."

"I followed my orders exactly, that is unquestionable."

"Yes, you did. You followed instruction to attack the camp and it was unsuccessful. Did you wonder about that at all?"

"Yes, of course I did. I know of strategy, what it takes to plan an attack. But Pinnacle Officer Cerberus is an engineer. Perhaps strategy is not his main concern. Nevertheless, I must follow the orders of the Pinnacle Officer, whether I agree with them or not."

"Perhaps they were designed in order for you to fail. Maybe we are just a distraction."

"You call this a distraction? 299 is expired! My best Fighters are expired! How is this a mere distraction?"

"The real orders were given after you left. The scroll I saw... It was not meant for you."

"Then who..."

"I do not know. But I know the orders that were given."

"Tell me. I must know, 201."

"The backup plan was simple, Reno. Destroy it. Destroy it all. You were not sent to be victorious in attacking the camp. Your purpose was only to pinpoint its location so it could be destroyed. They're going to burn the camp with you in it. They can't have any loose threads."

# 39

The next morning, Kap knocked on the door to the cabin, poking his head inside. The sunlight streamed in through the doorway, illuminating the tips of the straw.

"Raf wants to see you," he said.

201 squinted up at him, edging her way up the wall. "I thought Raf didn't want to speak with me."

"Alright then, Cal wants to see you, which means Raf wants to see you, it's the same thing. You coming or not?"

"Reno comes or I don't."

Reno shook his head. "201, what are you saying? Go with them!"

"No, Reno must come. I can vouch for him."

Kap let out a throaty laugh. "Vouch for him? Who will vouch for you? Nobody trusts you here, not after what happened."

"It matters not," said 201. "He's coming with me, unless you think you can't control the both of us."

Kap narrowed his eyes, grinning at 201's challenge. "Come on then, both of you. I think I can manage. Raf's not going to like it though, so I don't know, keep yourselves in check. Think you can remember that?"

"Lead the way," said 201 as they filed out the door.

# 40

201 blinked into the sunshine, trying to shield her face with her still-bound hands. Reno bumped into her shoulder, grunting in surprise.

"Why did you stop?" he asked.

"Look at that," she whispered.

A tiny blue bird with a forked tail sat on a branch outside their cabin. Its song was pleasing, bright and jarring at the same time. The bird cocked its head to the side, studying 201. It tittered, flicking its head this way and that before losing interest. 201 had encountered birds before from the vantage point in her chambers, staring out through the thin sliver of window at the forest below. She had even spotted them through the branches through the wooden bars of the cart, but she had never seen one up close like this. Its eyes blinked in rapid succession, the song bursting forth from its little chest as it puffed out its feathers to appear larger than its delicate frame. Before long another bird answered the call with a similar sound, the bird tilting its head to the side and calling to the other. 201 listened to their exchange, much like a conversation but with sounds instead of words.

"Come on," said Kap. "Raf will think we got lost."

201 looked up to catch the bird's departure. She was left gaping at the speed at which it disappeared without a sign of where it had landed. She stared at the now empty branch, still bobbing from the absence of weight. Kap opened the door to the main cabin, ushering them inside. Reno gave one last glance at 201, his brow furrowed. She turned to face Lina and Jotha, keeping watch by the door.

"201?" said Caltha. Her form was huddled in front of the fire, though the day was mild. She sat, wrapped in layers of blankets, face pale save for the flush of her cheeks.

201 moved towards her but was stopped by Rafaella's hand.

"That's close enough," said Rafaella, glancing over 201's shoulder. "What's he doing here?"

"She insisted," said Kap. "I couldn't really say no."

"No," said Rafaella, studying 201's face. "I suppose you couldn't." She remained standing between 201 and Caltha. "Say what you've got to say and then I want you out of here."

"Raf..." Caltha pulled the blankets from around her chin. "Let her through."

"No, Cal, you need to rest."

"Raf! Let her through."

Rafaella dropped her hand from 201's arm, grumbling as she stepped aside. "I'm watching you," she said as 201 stepped past her to kneel at Caltha's side.

"Caltha," said 201. "I am Beth 259201. It's good to finally meet you."

Caltha turned her head, attempting a smile. "I know who you are, 201," she said, adjusting the blankets. "I saw you." She lowered her voice to a whisper. "I saw you when I was there, with Renn. It was dark, but you were there. Thank you for being there."

"You're welcome," said 201. "I'm just glad you're okay." 201 placed a hand on Caltha's shoulder.

"That's enough. Cal needs to rest." Rafaella ushered 201 away from Caltha, leading her back to stand with Reno.

"Let them go," said Caltha.

"We've talked about this, Cal, it's too much of a risk."

"It's all I ask. Let them go."

Rafaella turned to face 201 and Reno. She huffed out a breath. "Give me one good reason why I should let you go."

201 stepped forward. "I believe in what you are doing here. I wish to fight against FERTS. To the end."

Rafaella studied 201's face. "Hmm. Is that so." She turned to Reno. "And what about you? What's your story?"

Reno cleared his throat. "I... was wrong. I would like the chance to make things right somehow."

"I don't know why I should believe either of you, but..."

"Raf..." said Caltha.

"I must be out of my... okay, fine. You got it. You'll have supervision but you can go free throughout the camp. I can't let you leave so that's the best I can do. Happy now?" she turned to Caltha.

Caltha just smiled, shifting to make herself more comfortable.

"So," said Rafaella. "What do you want to do first?" she looked over at Reno.

"I would like a tour of the camp. Maybe check out the weapons..."

"Ha," said Rafaella. "You hear that? The weapons."

"I'm curious, that's all."

"About our techniques? I'll bet you are. Not that your techniques aren't good, just... well, I'm not giving away our secrets to just anyone."

"I think 201 has proved..." began Reno.

"Proved what? You attacked our camp! What do you expect me to do?"

201 caught Jotha's eye. "I would like to bathe," she said. Jotha nodded, rummaging in a closet for some clothes for 201.

"201 has convinced me. I do not wish to fight you," said Reno.

"You say that now. Look what happened to Cal," said Rafaella.

"I didn't know."

"You didn't know? What's the matter with you? Can't you see what we face here? You don't get to see what we see. All you know is that place. Do you want to meet Zeta Circuit? I'm sure they would love to meet an Officer of FERTS!"

"Did you not listen to a word I said?" Reno threw his arms up in frustration. "I do not want to change your training methods, I just wish to observe."

"You do not know how to train an army. You may know how to run a show…"

"How dare you!" shouted Reno. Jotha edged past him, handing 201 a bundle of clothing. They stepped from the entrance of the main cabin, leaving the raised voices of Reno and Rafaella behind them.

"Is he always like that?" Jotha asked.

"Hmm. I suppose he is. What about Raf?"

"Yes, she is always like that. They should get along well." Jotha chuckled to himself, leading 201 down the path.

"I wanted to thank her," said 201 as they reached the edge of the waterfall. "What she did… it was something beautiful," 201 mused, watching Jotha as he folded her new clothing, placing it on a dry rock. "She saved them. You all did. Every one of them would not be here. You gave them something that they never had, never thought they would ever receive. Her plan, the rescue, it was a success."

"That was no rescue, 201." Jotha patted the clothing, backing away from the waterfall. "We're building an army."

Jotha headed for a large rock, seating himself with his back to 201.

"Take your time," he said. "I'll be here when you get out." He pulled a stick from the ground and began to whittle the end. "There's soap next to the clothes. You might need it."

"Thank you." 201 removed her Omega jumpsuit, wrinkling her nose at the stench of sweat and blood. She tossed it to the side, watching Jotha from the corner of her eye. He made no move to look at her, keeping his attention trained between the pathway to the waterfall and his task of whittling.

201 took a deep breath, taking in the scenery. The fragrance of the flowers surrounded her, underpinned by a fresh, mossy smell. 201 breathed deeply, absorbing the energies around her, revitalizing her entire being. She did not know how long she remained at the waterfall. Time slowed and sped up but 201 took no notice. She was in her own form, her own energies, no longer open to outside forces.

She grasped the soap and stood under the spray of the water, washing herself randomly, deliberately avoiding any reminder of bathing in regulation order. The soap was crudely made, with an earthy, minty fragrance. She shook her head under the stream, listening to the hiss of the cascading droplets spraying against moss and rocks. When she was done, she placed the soap on a rock and plunged into the water. She dived to the bottom of the pool, running her hands against reeds and watching the ripples distort the water above her, surrounding her with dappled sunlight.

201 rose to the surface, drifting towards the light.

She broke the surface with a gasp. The sun streamed across her face and the scent of wild flowers drifted along the surface of the water. She spied her Omega jumpsuit crumpled on a rock. A bird called from above. She turned to find the new pants and tunic and waiting for her, a leather belt placed on top. She chanced another peek at Jotha, who had barely moved from his spot on the rock, his attention trained on the finely whittled point at the end the stick. She sensed that he had not glanced in her direction in all the time she had been bathing. Not once.

She pulled the hair from her eyes, blinking the water from her vision. She was no longer an Internee of Epsilon, no longer an Internee of Omega, no longer an Internee of FERTS. She left the soiled Omega jumpsuit on the rock, pulling on her new clothing. She fastened the tunic, pulling the leather belt tight.

"I'm ready," she said.

Jotha put down his stick, tucking his knife in his boot.

She hopped down from the rock, shaking her hair until droplets rained down on her tunic. She felt new, cleansed and refreshed. Her spirit lifted as another bird called to her from the trees, the waterfall pattering against the moss, filling the air with mist.

The words of 232 rose in her mind and she felt her chest expand with the fresh scent of wild flowers.

*Someday I believe we, all of us, will be...*

She grabbed her soiled clothing and soap, following Jotha as he made his way back down the path towards the cabins.

*Free.*

Other books in this series:

FERTS
The Rogue Thread
Alpha Field


Other books by this author:

Demon Veil
Open Doors


Sign up to the Grace Hudson newsletter:
www.gracehudson.net

Twitter: @gracehudsonau

Facebook: www.facebook.com/gracehudsonauthor

Goodreads: www.goodreads.com/gracehudson

Manufactured by Amazon.ca
Bolton, ON